PRAIS
FROM SE\

"A brilliant story."
—*CanLit for Little Canadians* blog

"An exciting story [with] a lot of hearty laughs."
—*CM Magazine*

"Clever in its execution and wise in its thematic treatment." —*Resource Links*

PRAISE FOR *THE WOLF AND ME* FROM *THE SEVEN SEQUELS*

"Playfully and smartly written...An all-around rollicking read." —*Resource Links*

"Bunny's indomitable spirit makes him a likable, one-of-a-kind narrator...Readers will respond to this improbable, deeply sympathetic hero."
—*Kirkus Reviews*

"We are compelled to read on and on...If that isn't the mark of a good book, I don't know what is."
—*CM Magazine*

WEERDEST DAY EVER!

RICHARD SCRIMGER

ORCA BOOK PUBLISHERS

Library and Archives Canada Cataloguing in Publication

Scrimger, Richard, 1957–, author
Weerdest day ever / Richard Scrimger.
(The seven prequels)

Issued in print and electronic formats.
ISBN 978-1-4598-1155-3 (paperback).—ISBN 978-1-4598-1156-0 (pdf).—
ISBN 978-1-4598-1157-7 (epub)

I. Title.
PS8587.C745W44 2016   jC813'.54   C2016-900484-8
C2016-900485-6

First published in the United States, 2016
Library of Congress Control Number: 2016933651

Summary: In this middle-grade novel, Bunny ends up caught in a reenactment
of the War of 1812 while searching for a stolen cell phone.

*Orca Book Publishers is dedicated to preserving the environment and has
printed this book on Forest Stewardship Council® certified paper.*

Orca Book Publishers gratefully acknowledges the support for its publishing
programs provided by the following agencies: the Government of Canada
through the Canada Book Fund and the Canada Council for the Arts,
and the Province of British Columbia through the BC Arts Council
and the Book Publishing Tax Credit.

Design by Teresa Bubela
Cover photography by iStock.com
Author photo by Mark Raynes Roberts

ORCA BOOK PUBLISHERS
www.orcabook.com

Printed and bound in Canada.

19 18 17 16 • 4 3 2 1

To my nephews Nat and Cory

CREEKSIDE SCHOOL REPORT

SUBJECT, GRADE: *ENGLISH 10*
TEACHER, ROOM: *MR. WING, HALL D*
ASSIGNMENT: *WRITE A STORY ABOUT TIME WITH A FAMILY MEMBER.*
EXAMPLES: *FISHING WITH DAD, MY COUSIN'S BIRTHDAY PARTY, A VISIT WITH GRANDMA, BABYSITTING MY SISTER*
TIPS: *SET UP YOUR STORY. MAKE SURE THERE IS A PROBLEM. USE COMMAS AND QUOTATION MARKS IN YOUR DIALOGUE. REMEMBER—GOOD WRITING COMES FROM THE MIND AND THE HEART!*

YOUR NAME: Bunny O'Toole
YOUR STORY TITLE: WEERDEST DAY EVER!

THIS STORY IS TRUE—

most of it. Some parts I will have to make up because I dont remember every word people said way back then. But mostly its true. You wont think so but it is. Like the war. Yah there reely was a war. Or the...

BEGIN YOUR STORY ON THE NEXT PAGE

Oops. Sorry.

THIS STORY IS TRUE—

most of it. Some parts I will have to make up because I dont remember every word people said way back then. But mostly its true. You wont think so but it is. Like the war. Yah there reely was a war. Or the cow. Or the hollow tree. Or what happened to the 1 arm man. That was funny all rite.

It all happened a while ago. Im in Grade 10 now and this was back at the end of Grade 6 so—that long ago. Grampa took me and Spencer camping. No one else. No Mom and Dad or the other cousins. Just Grampa and me and my brother.

Thats what this story is about. We stayed over night but it was Saturday afternoon and Sunday morning so it was really only 1 day. I culd call it My Day With Grampa or My Day With Spencer. Only I didn't see much of them and some reely weerd things happened. I mean *really weerd.* So Im calling it Weerdest Day Ever! I think thats the rite title.

OK I will start now.

* * *

Grampa picked us up from our house in Toronto and drove us to Queen something Park. That was the name of the park. I dont know where it was. It took us all morning to get there. We drove over a long bridge and went left and the sun hit me where I was sitting in the back of the Jeep.

Did I say it was the week end? It was. Almost summer so it was warm enuff for short pants. I wore one of Dad's old t shirts. It said *BREAD* on it. Thats all—*BREAD.* Dad said I looked groovy. Then he laffed. Spencer wore baggy shorts with lots of pockets and zips. He hated them because they made his legs look skinny.

"But your legs are skinny," I said.

Spencer is a year older than me but Im bigger.

"Theyre even skinnier in these stupid shorts," he said.

By now we were in the park and driving slow. I was eating ice cream. There was a place out side the park gates and we stopped there for lunch. Spencer had finished his ice cream. He sat back and frowned at all the trees. He doesnt like camping. I do. Camping means sleeping in a tent and cooking on a fire. Fun you know? Spencer doesnt think so. Hes smarter than me and he likes inside things. Reading comic books and gaming. And his new phone. He loves that.

I better say rite now—Spencer is not the only one who is smarter than me. This is in case you cant tell already. Just about every body is smarter than me. My class—my family—every body. I saw a video with a chicken who culd always tell witch cup had the little ball under it. No matter how they mixed up the 3 cups the chicken wuld always peck at the one with the ball. I culdn't do it and I was watching the video. I figure that chicken is smarter than me. Not much smarter because I can tie my skates and count—but a bit smarter.

This is in case you want better spelling. Im doing my best. I have trouble with lots of words—2 and to and real and reel. And a hole bunch more. I go with the way they sound even tho I know some words are weerd. Like is it frend or freind? Let me check. Oh.

I will forget that.

Anyway. We drove on a bumpy road along the outside of the park. After a few minutes we found an open place to put up our tents. 2 tents. I was going to be with Spencer and Grampa was by himself. That was a good thing. Have you ever slept near an old person? They fart a lot and go *whhhhhh* and *unnnnnnng*. You know? And they moan and smell like mint and teeth.

6

When the tents were up Grampa and I went to get wood and then he took us for a walk and told us the rules. Grampa was big on rules. He was going to let me and Spencer be on our own but he wanted us to stay close and check in. That was the rule for this trip.

"Do you understand Bernard?" he asked.

Grampa was the only one who called me Bernard. Every body else called me Bunny.

"Will I trust you Bernard?"

"I dont know," I said.

I mean you cant tell what some one else will do.

Grampa frowned.

"Let me ask again. Will I trust you Bernard? I want to trust you."

I looked at Spencer for help but he was busy checking his pockets.

"You shuld do what you want Grampa," I said. "Unless it hurts somebody."

Thats my rule. Its a pretty good rule.

Grampa looked at me a long time. I looked back. I don't know what Spencer did. There was shouting in the distance and a sound like banging on a pot.

"OK I will trust you both," said Grampa. "I want you to have fun here. Pay attention. This is not a normal weekend at the park. There will be surprises."

More shouting and a boom sound. Fire works maybe. Cool.

"Like a birthday party? That kind of surprise?"

"Youll find out Bernard."

Spencer grabbed my arm. "Theres a problem," he said.

SPENCERS BEST THING

in the hole world was his phone. He liked it more than his glasses or his best jeans or his Star Wars action guys or—or anything. It was bran new for his birthday and it did lots of things. He culd watch movys on his phone or play games or tell time or do math. He culd look up stuff on the internet. He culd even make phone calls.

It was a smart phone he told me.

I agreed. I didnt know if his phone culd pick out a ball under a cup like the chicken in the video. But it sounded pretty smart.

Mom told Spencer to be careful of his phone. She made him get a safe plastic case for it. She told him to leave it home this weekend. Spencer took it anyway. He liked it 2 much to leave it home.

"Dont tell Mom," he said to me in his room.

"OK," I said.

"I mean it. This phone is my life," he said. He zipped it into his pocket.

"OK."

And now the phone was gone.

That was the problem. So I went xploring by myself. The woods were thick and the path was bumpy. There were more bangs. I smelled fire works and headed for them. Fire works are fun.

I slowed down when I came up to the guys with guns.

Thats what I said. Guns. There were a bunch of guys—like 6 or 8 of them—in a small open area ahead of me. And they had guns. Not pistols like cops or gangs use. These were rifles—only longer and fancy looking.

That was the smell. Not fire works. Guns.

I dropped strait down so the gun guys wuldnt see me. Then I crawled inside a bush.

One of them was yelling at the others. He didnt have a gun. "Fire lock!" he shouted. Then something about a cart ridge. Then he yelled, "Prime!"

Whatever that ment.

He was the boss. He was in charge. He shouted while the other guys played with the guns. They clicked some thing on the sides of the guns and then pored stuff into the tops—the gun barrels. "Rammer!" he shouted. I think that was it. The guys stuck poles into the guns. Reely. Inside them.

Then the boss said, "Sholder." You know—like the part of your body. Sholder. The guys all lifted the guns to there sholders.

I didnt get it. There was nothing here. They were pointing the guns at nothing. They looked like they were in a gang or an army but I didnt know who they were fiting. There was no body there xept squirrels maybe.

No wait—there was a woman with a video camera! She was filming the guys with the guns. Did they see her? Did they know? They didnt look at her. They kept pointing guns at the maybe squirrels.

She wore jeans and sandals. She looked normal.

"Fire!" shouted the boss guy. Did I say he had a sord? He did. They were all dressed in blue coats and white pants and tall hats but the boss had a sord insted of a gun.

As soon as he said *Fire* there was a bunch of bangs as loud as thunder. Reely. Or louder. Like if you dropped a mountain made out of glass. That loud. My ears hurt. The smoke was thick as a blanket. You culdnt hear or see any thing for a while.

Weerd.

Maybe I shuld of been scared but I wasnt. Or not much. Yah it was loud and all—but the guys werent shooting at me. They werent shooting at any body. I didnt get it. And why were they dressed in funny clothes? I didnt get that ether.

And what about the video woman? Was she from the CBC or some place? Was this going to be on the news tonite?

I didn't get any of this.

Of course I was used to not getting stuff. Math. Or games. Spencer tried to teach me chess. He showed me how the horse moved—up and then over—and I just laffed.

"Reely?" I asked and he said, "Reely." I laffed some more.

When I dont understand something I just go "OK then" inside. Thats what I did now. Guns and sords and cameras? OK then. The smoke was every where. I stayed in my bush until Beth and Tyler came.

I DIDNT KNOW WHO THEY WERE YET.

They stood next to where I was hiding and stared down the path at the backs of the blue and white guys with the guns.

"Thats an American patrol," said Beth. She was a kid about my age with long hair in a brade down her back. "Did you hear them talk? They sound American. You cant always tell. Some times Americans sound like us. But not these guys."

Maybe my age. Maybe a little older. Her skin was smooth and brown like wet toffee.

Tyler nodded and didnt say anything. His skin was darker than hers. I didnt like him.

"Lets follow," said Beth. "We can sneak up on them. OK? Itll be good practice for tomorrow."

Tyler nodded and bent down low. I didnt know his name yet ether. Or that he was Beths brother. She bent 2. Now there faces were rite next to mine. Both of them wore make up.

"Hi," I said from inside my bush.

Beth made a noise like *eeech!*

Tyler didnt say anything.

I crawled out of the bush and stood up. We looked at each other. Tyler had no shirt and no hair xept for a strip down the top of his head with a fether in it. I saw now that Beth had a fether in her hair 2. They both wore soft lether pants with a frill—no frinj thats the word. Frinj. Beths shirt had a frinj 2. Their make up was dark brown stripes across their cheeks like this == Like equals in math you know? 2+2==4.

This was something else weerd—something else I did not understand. These guys with fethers and make up were like the guys and the guns and the video camera. OK then.

I told them my name.

"Im Bunny," I said. "Who are you?"

She ansered. Thats when I found out their names.

"Im Beth and this is my brother Tyler," she said. "Were both in grade 6. He has a different mom but hes still my brother."

We nodded at each other.

I liked Tyler better now that I knew he was Beths brother. I said hi and that I was in grade 6. Beth said hi.

"Dont mind Tyler," she told me. "He listens good but he doesnt say much."

Tyler nodded. I nodded 2.

"Were with the British," said Beth.

"Huh?"

"From Canada you know? In the battle tomorrow. Were fiting the Americans."

This was a big deal. I didnt understand but I culdnt just keep going and think OK then.

"Woe!" I said. And then I said, "What?"

"Didnt you know?"

"I didnt know we were at war with America," I said.

War with America! It xplaned the camera any way. People wuld want to know how the war was going. And it xplaned the guns. You cant fite a war without guns.

"Not today. Tomorrow," said Beth. "Tomorrow is the war."

I was still getting my mind around it. War. I shuld tell Grampa and Spencer about this. Theyd want to get out of here early if there was going to be a war.

Tyler and Beth didnt seem very worried.

"Lets follow the American patrol," she said. "You can come with us Bunny. You want to? Come on. They went this way. Can you see them Tyler?"

He took a tube out of his pocket and put it up to his face.

"Thats a—what is that again?"

"Telescope," said Beth. "Its Tylers. Dad got it for him last year. Cool eh?"

"Yah."

Tyler put the telescope away and waved his arm down the path.

"The Americans must be a long way away," said Beth. "Lets go."

No more sneaking. They ran down the path. I ran after them.

"War?" I said. "Reely? War?"

Tyler looked over at me and nodded firmly.

War. I didnt understand but it seemed to be happening.

Wow.

It was still a big deal.

I looked up as we ran. I culd see a bit of sky thru the tops of the trees. If America was fiting us tomorrow there mite be planes now. Checking things out. I didnt see any. Maybe the Canadian Air Force was keeping the sky safe.

Maybe.

There was no body on the path but us. Not even squirrels. There was noise up ahead getting louder. A different kind of banging—like pots and pans not fire works.

"The Americans must be in the town," said Beth.

The path got wider. We slowed down.

"Isnt this fun Bunny?" Beth asked. "Our dad fites a lot of weekends in the summer. Thats why were here."

"Your dad?"

"Yah he loves fiting. He says war is the noblest thing you can do. He loves being a hero. And he usually is. Eh Tyler?"

Tyler nodded. His eyes were shiny black and flat. Like wet stones or water melon seeds.

I culdnt think of my dad fiting anyone. And he sure didnt like me fiting. Not even if I was rite. Like when Mean Ali wanted all my M n Ms. I was rite then and Dad was unhappy.

Mean Ali is a big guy in grade 8 with a drippy nose. Nobody likes him. Theres another Ali in our school. Every body calls him Smiling Ali because—well you can guess why. Last month Mean Ali wanted some of my M n Ms so I gave him some but then he wanted more.

He grabbed at the box. I pulled it out of his way and he tried to kick me. He fell on his back when I grabbed his shoe and held on to it. This all happened in the lunch room. Mean Ali ended up on the floor. The lunch lady was mad! She took us both to the office and we got sent home. Mean Alis mom dragged him away. My dad shook his head at me.

"Fiting is wrong," he said.

"Always?" I said.

"Give peace a chance," he said.

I dont know about that. I gave Mean Ali a chance. And he kicked me.

* * *

"Our dads famous," said Beth. "He's the reason the British win. His name's Tecumseth. He's the best general in the hole war."

"Tecumseth!" I said. "Your dad is Tecumseth?"

"You know him?"

"I live on Tecumseth," I said. "Tecumseth Ave. Thats my house. Its in Toronto. Are you saying my street is named after your dad? That is pretty cool."

Its also how come I can spell it. All those times riting my address—2 Tecumseth Ave Toronto Ontario m5v 3h7.

The path ended at a big open place as big as 2 or 3 football fields. It was full of tents and wagons and people. There were 100s of people—maybe more. Also some horses and dogs. And a house made of logs like the pine ears used to live in. Old timey. The people looked old timey 2—they wore hats and long dresses and shoe buckles. And they were playing with weerd things. Hammers. Spinning wheels. Saws and axes. Like that. Like everyone had a hobby and was showing off the hobby you know? Like they made bird houses or blankets. Or natural honey. When we go to the market Dad always gets something from those honey guys.

"This is the town," said Beth.

"What town?"

"Just the town. Theres always a town. It doesnt have a name. Every body comes here. See—theres the American patrol we were following."

She pointed at some guys who stood around a fire eating. I guess they were the same guys. They were the same uniforms. Their guns were stacked in a circle near by.

People were taking pictures of the guns. Of course. The war was big news. I saw the movie camera woman again.

The town was full of uniforms—blue uniforms and red. I guess the red were our guys. If we were at war with America and the Americans were in blue then the red guys would be us. Its the same in hockey. We wear red and the Americans wear blue.

There were lots of guns and sords around but no body was fiting. Not yet anyway. Tomorrow was the fite.

I HAD to tell Grampa and Spencer about this. We were safe now but what about when the fiting started? What wuld happen to us then? We culd beat America in hockey sometimes. But culd we beat them in fiting? Maybe not.

Beth and Tyler were talking to me but I didnt hear. Well Beth was talking.

"What?" I said.

"Do you want to meet him?"

"Who?"

"Dad. Come on."

She pulled me along. I let her.

Well I didnt want to fite her. And how culd I say no to meeting the guy my street was named for?

Her hand on my bare arm felt smooth.

MR TECUMSETH SAT AT A PICNIC TABLE BY HIMSELF.

He was polishing a sord. He was thin with a hooky kind of nose and long dark hair. The sord was curved and had a handle with a silver nob. Grampa has a sord 2—Ive seen it. Its got blood on it. He took it off a guy a long time ago.

Mr Tecumseth wore a red uniform and had a fether in his hair. Like Tyler and Beth. He looked younger than my dad and older 2—like he knew more things. He stood up and shook my hand. Hey he was short—not much taller than me. But he stood reel strait and still so he looked taller. Tyler stood next to him. They looked like each

24

other—apart from Tyler being younger. Huh. I wondered if I look like my dad.

"I live on your street," I said.

"I beg your pardon young man?"

"My street is called Tecumseth," I said.

He smiled. "It is good that we remember our heroes," he said.

"Like you."

"Like Tecumseth."

His voice was deep—a TV news guy voice. You know what I mean. They all talk way down here. Even if the news guy is a woman. News is important. Sports and wether guys dont have deep voices because that stuff doesnt matter. Partly cloudy with a chance of showers—so what?

Speaking of important news I had to ask Mr Tecumseth.

"Are you worryed about tomorrow?" I said. "About war with America. Theyre a bigger country than us."

He shook his head. "We will win tomorrow," he said.

"But what if we dont?"

"We will win."

He sounded like my soccer coach who said we wuld beat St Marys even tho they were a way better team than us. "Shout it!" he told us at haff time. "We will win! We will win! We will win!"

We were already losing 2-0. We looked at each other and said, "We will win!"—but we knew we wuldnt.

And we didnt.

Mr Tecumseth sat back down. His table was out of the way. There were other tables set up to sell stuff and make stuff. It was kind of a street of tables. People walked up and down the street pointing at things. Nobody looked worryed. I reely didnt understand. Were they all as sure of them selves as Mr Tecumseth? Didnt any body know how big America was?

"Cool sord," I said to Mr Tecumseth.

He nodded up at me. "And its real. It was used in a real war."

Well of course it was. Sords are for fiting. Of course his sord was used.

Another guy came over. He was in a blue uniform—an American. Witch made him a bad guy. Thats why I watched him. And because he had 1 arm. I mean only 1. The other was gone. He tucked that sleeve of his blue coat into his pocket. You dont see a lot of 1 arm guys. I didnt want to be rude so I peeked and then looked away.

He was fat but hard. Bully fat not fatso fat. He had a curly mustash that stuck way out. He was eating an ice cream cone carefully—making sure he didnt get any on his mustash.

He was important to the story but I didnt know that yet.

"Ha ha ha," he said. "The big bad Indians."

His voice grated like there was sand in it. His smile wasnt a nice smile. His teeth were 2 sharp in his mouth.

Mr Tecumseth looked up quick. "Oh its you," he said. "Your a major this weekend."

The major smiled harder. "Your still a red skin," he said. "Going to get a lot of scalps with that sord—you savage?"

Mr Tecumseth didnt do anything but I was so shocked I spoke out loud.

"Thats not fair," I said. Witch is what I said to Mean Ali when he wanted more M n Ms. "Calling names is mean," I said to the major. "Savage is a bad name."

He went *whhhhoop* and swelled like a balloon. You culd see him filling with air.

"Thats what they said in 1812. Its a joke. Same when I call him a red skin. Ha ha."

"But hes a hero," I said. "With a street named after him."

There was a minute of silence. You know how that happens. No body can decide what to say so the hole room is quiet. People streamed past us but our little group around the table was quiet. And in the quiet I herd the buzz from a phone. Spencers phone did that when somebody sent him a text. I herd it driving down with Grampa.

Spencer had the phone noise turned off so Grampa culdnt hear but I was sitting next to him in the Jeep and I herd the buzzing. And now I herd it again.

The 1 arm major jumped and put his hand on his pocket. So I knew the buzzing was his phone. But he didnt anser. He finished his cone and wiped his mustash and turned to me with a twisted face.

"You dont look like a redskin kid," he said. "Are you part of the battle?"

"I hope not," I said. "Im going to tell my grampa so we miss the fiting."

"But thats why we are here—to fite. Dont you know that? How stupid are you?"

"Pretty stupid," I said. "I always have been. How come your such a bully? Is it from when you were little? Is that why?"

Dad xplaned that to me about Mean Ali.

"Did the kids in your class pick on you?" I asked the major. "Were your mom and dad mean? Is that why your mean 2?"

"I—"

He started and stopped. Mr Tecumseth choked. He mite of been laffing.

The major tried again.

"You have no idea—"

He stopped again.

"Your as much of a savage as them!" he said to me. He made a fist and shook it at me. Reely he did—like a bad guy in a Bugs Bunny cartoon. Then he turned to Mr Tecumseth. "Enjoy your sord—hero!" he said. And marched off into the crowd.

THERE WAS ANOTHER
LITTLE SILENCE AROUND US.

"Dad," said Beth finally. "Who is that guy? I dont like him at all. And what did he mean about enjoying your sord?"

Mr Tecumseth shook his head sadly.

"I ran into him last summer," he said. "He led his men into my ambush. His sord broke in half because it was made out of wood and his men laffed at him."

"Wow!" I said. "A wood sord. Thats almost as bad as card bord."

In our school play last year the guys all had card bord sords. The Prince and the Something was the name of the play. The guys broke the sords in practice. The teacher was mad.

"And now he hates you? And your sord?"

"He wants what I have," said Mr Tecumseth. "He teases me to feel better about himself."

Just like Mean Ali. At least thats what Dad said. Huh.

"But how come he can call you a savage?" I asked. "How is that OK?"

"Its not OK Bunny," said Mr Tecumseth in his deep voice. "But a long time ago lots of people wuld of called us savages. That major can pretend its OK this weekend."

I tried to understand.

"Because of the war?" I asked.

"Yes Bunny. Because of the war."

"He called me a savage 2," I said.

"Yah. He was mean to you Bunny," said Beth. She turned to her dad. "Why didnt you say something to help?"

Mr Tecumseth smiled. "Bunny didnt need any help," he said.

Tyler normally didnt change his face much. But he was smiling too. He came over to me and clapped like he was at a show.

Clapping was his way of saying thank you.

"Your welcome," I said.

He bent his finger at me and pointed at a tree beside the table. He walked his fingers upward—he was asking if I wanted to clime the tree.

"Sure," I said.

Tyler clapped again and ran over to the tree and jumped to grab the lowest branch. I did the same thing and we climed together. It wasnt an ever green tree—it was the other kind. Witch ment that there were no sharp needles and the branches werent bunched together. You culd see a long way when you got close to the top. Looking around I saw a river and another river and a lake. I saw a plane high over head. Was it a jet fiter or a bomber? I culdnt tell. It looked like a regular plane.

Tyler had his telescope up to his face. He was staring down at the far end of the town.

"Whats going on?" I asked.

He past the telescope over—holding on to it an extra second so I knew how much he liked it and how careful he wanted me to be. "OK," I said. "Dont worry."

With the telescope every thing looks closer. There was a stage set up at the far end of the town. A girl sat on stage under a bucket. She wore a long dress. The bucket tipped upside down and splashed the girl with water and she jumped. I saw the hole thing. I saw her mouth open in a scream. Every body on the ground was laffing.

The telescope was gold—well it was metal with a gold color. It was cool all rite. I was about to hand it back to Tyler when I saw the 1 arm man in the crowd. He stood near the stage. He was laffing pretty hard at the wet girl. Then he stopped laffing and put his hand in his pants pocket.

He looked around—slow and cool like he wanted to make sure no body was watching. Then he walked away from the crowd looking over his sholder. Weerd or what? He looked just like a spy—or a guy doing some thing he didnt want any body to see. I watched him with Tylers telescope. When he was by himself he took out his phone and looked at it.

I almost fell out of the tree.

Thats how surprised I was.

I grabbed a smooth branch to stop from falling. I checked again. I said it out loud.

"The 1 arm man has Spencers phone," I said.

IN THE TELESCOPE I
CULD SEE

the phone. It was easy to see thanks to the cover. The cover for Spencers phone is pretty silly. Mom made him get a cover in case he dropped it and she picked the britest. Spencer loves his phone but not the cover. It is yellow. SO yellow! Like a school bus is yellow or an egg yoke. Like the sun. Thats how yellow.

You can see Spencers phone from down the block. I never saw any body else with that cover. No body but Spencer has that cover.

And there it was in the telescope.

Tyler looked me a question. His eyes got wider and his hands went up like—Whats going on?

I xplaned.

"Remember the mean guy with 1 arm?" I said. Tyler nodded. "Remember he was eating an ice cream cone?" I said. Tyler nodded. "That's where he got it," I said.

Tylers hands went up again. Fingers spread out and shaking like he was asking What?

"The phone," I said. "My brother left his phone at the ice cream place and the guy picked it up with his 1 arm. I mean with his 1 hand. I mean the guy with 1 arm picked up the phone."

I was upset and not making a lot of sense.

I gave the telescope back to Tyler. He looked thru it. Frowned. Shrugged. Shook his head.

"Didnt you see it?"

I took back the scope. Culdnt see the guy any more. He and his lonely arm were lost in the crowd. I didnt think what to do. I knew.

I had to get Spencers phone back. Yes there were other things to do 2—like warn Grampa about war with America so we culd get out of here. But I had to get Spencers phone first or hed be in so much trouble hed never get out. Look after each other said Grampa. This phone is my life said Spencer. OK Id look after Spencer—save his life. Then me and him and Grampa culd get out of here before the fiting started tomorrow.

I dropped down the tree like a monkey and said good by to Mr Tecumseth and Beth.

I asked him what he knew about the 1 arm man.

"Apart from being a jerk," I said.

"Hes American," said Mr Tecumseth. "I mean reely American—not just for the fiting tomorrow."

"Why wuld he steel my brothers phone?"

"Phone?"

"I saw it," I said.

I xplaned about the telescope.

"He shuldnt have the phone," said Mr Tecumseth.

"I know," I said. "Its not his."

"But a phone is wrong," said Mr Tecumseth. "What if the phone rang in the middle of the battle? It wuld ruin everything."

I didnt get that. A phone call culd be a reel help. You culd find out where the bad guys were or where to look for help.

Mr Tecumseth saw how confused I was. He shook his head. "There were no cell phones in 1812," he said.

I nodded like—duh.

Why was he telling me that? I was not smart but I knew some things. I knew about Alexander Grame Bell and Dr Watson. I knew that if you wanted to phone somebody in 1812 you had to dial. Dr Watson wuld get a call from Sherlock Homes but not on a cell phone. "Watson come here I want you," Sherlock wuld say and Watson wuld come over.

I knew this stuff.

"So a phone call in the fite tomorrow wuld be a mistake," said Mr Tecumseth.

"Well," I said. "If the phone rang he wuldnt have to anser."

Mr Tecumseth had finished polishing his sord so he put it on and walked over to where a guy with huge mussels was holding a horse by its leg and trying to hammer on a horse shoe. Horse shoes are supposed to be lucky but this horse didnt look like it was having much fun. It stamped its other feet one after the other.

Mr Tecumseth walked over to help. He was way shorter than the horse but he wasnt scared. He talked to it in his TV news voice and the horse shook its head and started to calm down. The mussels guy said thank you and pounded away. Mr Tecumseth looked like a hero all rite. The sort of guy who wuld have a street named after him.

Tyler was down from the tree. I told him thanks for letting me look thru his telescope. He flipped his hand to show it was no problem.

"Where are you going Bunny?" said Beth.

"To look for the 1 arm man," I said. "He has my brothers phone."

"Tyler and I can help," she said. "We can all spread out and look. That way we can check more places."

That made sense.

"You dont have to," I said.

"We want to help you. The 1 arm man called us savages. Didnt he Tyler? Do you want to help Bunny?"

Tyler nodded hard. His head went way up and way down. He reely wanted to help.

"OK lets go," I said. Tyler and I started out.

"Wait."

Beth had her arms out. "Lets have a plan," she said. "Its important to have a plan. Listen to me you guys. Ready to listen?"

Tyler and I stopped and looked at each other. He snapped his fingers like—Oh yah!

A plan made sense. Beth talked a lot but she was smart.

"Heres the plan," she said. "We each look on our own for a wile and then meet in front of the big red tent over there." She pointed.

"You cant miss it. Its down by the stream. Its the biggest tent on the hole site and its red. Its our head quarters for the fite tomorrow."

"Like the flag," I said.

"Eh?"

I shook my head. I knew what I ment. Our flag is red and white you know? I guess our head quarters would be red.

"And lets all try to find his tent," she said. "I mean the 1 arm major. Maybe he will put your brothers phone in his tent. Lets ask the Americans where the tent is. What do you think Tyler? What do you think Bunny?"

"Tent. Rite. That reminds me," I said and ran off.

"What?" she shouted after me. "What Bunny? What does it remind you of?"

"I'll be back," I shouted. "See you soon."

She was still talking when I got 2 far away 2 hear.

What she said about the majors tent reminded me of our tents. And that reminded me I shuld talk to Spencer and Grampa.

I had to tell Spencer about his phone and I had to warn Grampa about the war. I didnt know where they were so I decided to go to our tent. I went back the way I came. I ran through the woods and found the road and ran along it.

I was glad that Beth and Tyler were helping me. I liked them. Tyler didnt talk much but then nether did I. And Beth talked enuff for all of us.

I liked their clothes 2. Tylers hair and the fethers they all wore. And the soft lether pants. Cool. And their dad was Tecumseth. Super cool.

Why wuld anybody call them savages? I didnt get that. The 1 arm guy said it was all rite. I didnt get that ether.

OK then.

As I was walking I kept my eyes open for Spencer and Grampa and the 1 arm man. I didnt see any of them. I saw some nature—birds and squirrels and like that. I saw a horse far away. Or maybe it was a cow. I didnt know much about cows then. (I know more now—like they can be dangerous! Sorry. Thats not part of this story.)

I saw a jet heading across the sky with a trail behind it. It didnt come down to bomb us or the Americans. I guessed it was waiting until the next day. I saw hills and grass and water sparkling in the distance.

It was a nice day but I didnt reely enjoy it. I was worryed about the war and Spencers phone.

I found our 2 tents pretty easy. They looked like most of the others but they had our stuff in them. My sleeping bag was turned down like I left it. It was green on the outside and white on the inside with pictures of cowboys. Pretty lame I know. I picked it when Mom and I went shopping. Spencer has Star Wars.

He and Grampa were gone. I shouted but they didnt anser.

I found some paper and a crayon in my back pack and left a note for Spencer on top of his sleeping bag.

1 arm man has yore fone. Bunny.

Then I did a note for Grampa.

Bak sun. Bernard.

PS. There is a war! Shuld we go home?

I left the note on Grampas pillow. I put *Bernard* so he wuld know it was me.

I was not as good at spelling back then as I am now. Thats why the notes are not as well written as the rest of this.

YOU THINK I CULD FIND A GUY WITH 1 ARM

but I culdnt. I searched the town part of the camp site but didnt see him. I found a guy with only 1 leg. And a couple of guys with only 1 eye. But everyone I saw had 2 arms.

They were all having fun. Eating and drinking and laffing. There were lots of games where you throw things. Horse shoes and things like that. Or theyd roll a ball along the ground and then laff when it hit another ball.

Didnt they know? Why werent they worried? I tried to find my guy. Also I tried to warn people.

Like the family having the picnic. They had a blanket spread out on the ground and a cooler with ice and pop and sandwiches. The mom leaned against a tree. The 2 little kids ran around screaming. Dad told them to come back and finish lunch. Every body was smiling. Normal you know. I went up and asked if they had seen a man with 1 arm and they said no.

"Hes American," I said. "He has a mustash and a uniform and my brothers phone. It has a yellow cover."

"Sorry," said the mom. "I havent seen him."

She had an axent.

"Your American," I said.

"And proud of it," she said.

Oh oh I thought—an enemy. She didnt look like an enemy tho. Nether did the dad or the kids. They were little. Like kindergarten or younger. They came up and grabbed my legs—you know how kids do. They wore short pants and strappy shirts with no sleeves. I smelled sun block.

"Hey there," I said and patted their heads.

They wouldnt let me go.

The stage was near by. I dont know what was going on but the crowd was laffing.

The kids still wuldnt let go. They were cute but a pain. You know—little kids.

A guy rode by on a horse. It snorted and scared the kids. They screamed and hung on extra hard.

"See the horsy," said the mom. "What does the horsy say?"

"Hey!" I shouted. "Hey!"

"Thats what a horsy eats," said the dad. Mom laffed.

"No. No. There he is!" I said.

The 1 arm guy.

"Hey!" I yelled again.

I tried to get the little kids off my legs but they hung on hard.

The 1 arm guy was past us now, riding down toward the river. His hand was on the rains and he was looking around like he was the boss of every body. I followed him until he went behind some trees and vanished.

"Horsy," said one of the kids. The one on my left leg. "Play horsy!"

She giggled.

"Giddy up horsy," said the other kid. "Giddy up!"

"Whats your name?" asked the girl. When I told her she laffed and laffed. And laffed some more.

"Horsy is a bunny," she said.

"Bunny is a horsy," said the boy. He was laffing 2.

They laffed so hard they let go of my legs and rolled around on the grass.

I had to chase the 1 arm guy but first I wanted to warn this mom and dad.

"You know theres going to be fiting," I told them. "Tomorrow."

The dad smiled at me. "Uh huh. Thats why were here," he said.

"Real fiting. Sords and guns."

"Yah," said the dad. "Im in the first American attack."

A nice guy but an enemy. He asked if I wanted a juice box. The 2 kids were still laffing and rolling around. The sun was shining.

War is strange.

I left the nice American family and headed for where the 1 arm man had gone on his horse. Beth came running up to me.

"I saw him Bunny!" she said. "The 1 arm guy."

"Me 2," I said.

"He was on a big bay horse and he was headed down to the river. Lets go after him. Are you a good runner? I am. You shuld run like I do. I run every day for an hour. Well not xactly every day but most days. And maybe not a hole hour but most of an hour. I start running when *Cooking Wars* comes on and when I come back its over. I cant stand that show. The chefs face looks like a bowl of oat meal—you ever noticed? He smiles and its like the syrup leaks out of his skin and runs down his face and I go Ewww."

All this time we were running down to the river. Beth didnt stop talking until we got there.

Mom and Anti Vicki talk a hole lot but Beth was—well she was—wow.

Down by the river there was place with a fence around it and horses inside. What do you call that again? I didnt see anyone with 1 arm.

Beth was talking about her family. A gramma was this and another gramma was that and somebody married somebody so Beth was a lot of different kinds of things—part this and part that and part something else. I didnt know any of the words she said xept Mohawk. I knew that one.

Tylers haircut was a Mohawk. That strip down the middle.

"They say I dont look like one. What do you think?" Beth said.

"One what?"

"An Indian," she said. "Tyler looks like one. Dad does. But I dont look Indian at all. My dad says I look like a cheer leader. What do you think?"

I know. I know. Indians are from India. Mom and Dad told me and so did the teachers at school.

I didnt think Beth was from India but I wasnt going to tell her what she culd call herself. After all her dad was Tecumseth.

And of course she culd be a cheer leader. Cheer leaders can look like anybody cant they?

"I don't know," I said.

Beth was leading me closer to the horses and still talking. Core al—thats the word I was looking for. Core al. Where the horses were behind the fence.

The guy in charge of the horses was a kid like me or maybe a bit older. He wore a cowboy hat and spat a lot. I went up and asked him if hed seen a 1 arm man.

He spat pink—he was chewing bubble gum. Ew.

"Who wants to know?" he said.

I didnt get it. Who did he think? "Me," I said.

"And who are you?"

"My names Bunny."

He spat again. "So what?"

I didnt know if I liked him or not. Maybe he acted mean because he felt sick.

"Are you OK?" I asked.

"Shut up," he said. "Im better than you."

OK then. I didnt like him.

BETH WAS LEANING
OVER THE FENCE

to pet a horse. The guy saw her and waved.

"Hey Beth," he said.

She turned.

"Hey Clod."

They smiled at each other.

"Horses eat hay," I said. The same joke that the dad made to me. They didnt laff.

"I didnt recognize you in that hat Clod," said Beth. "Looks cool."

They knew each other from before. When she asked about the 1 arm guy he didnt say *Who wants to know.*

"Sure," said Clod. "He's got that big bay horse for the afternoon. He was just here asking about the south trail. Hes a good rider."

A woman rode up. Clod helped her down and led her horse into the core al.

Beth pulled me aside. "Did you hear that? The 1 arm man is on the south trail," she said. "We shuld follow him. I can ride a horse. Can you ride a horse? We shuld follow the trail until we catch site of him and then can creep up on him and find your brothers phone. Where do you think hes going? Can you trail ride? Can you jump a horse if you have to? Why dont you anser my questions?"

She was standing rite next to me. Her eyebrows went up and up.

"I dont know witch 1 to start with," I said.

Beth talked Clod into giving us 2 horses. My horse was named Gale. She was black xept for one foot so it looked like she was wearing a white sock.

"Gale—like the wind," said Clod. "Thats how she runs."

"Theres a girl in my class called Gale," I said. "But thats just her name. She doesnt run like the wind. Shes good at math tho."

Id never been on a horse before. It was like a ride at Wonderland—up and down and around. But you dont fall off the Wonderland ride and I did fall off the horse. And then I fell off again. Beth laffed. Clod laffed. Gale said, "Nay." This is horse talk but the way she said it made it sound like she was laffing too.

I finally did get on the horse by treating her like a hill and climbing up with my hands and feet. I spread out on top of her and hung on to the saddle and mane. My face hung down over one side of the horse. Clod and Beth laffed some more. Her horse was gray and she looked comfy in the saddle. Clod turned me round and told me to put my feet in the things where your feet go.

"Dont worry," Beth said to Clod. "I can look after Bunny. Youll get your horses back in an hour or so."

We walked down the path to the stream and splashed across. Beth told me to sit normally and think nice thots. "Horses are good at reading how you feel," she said. "They know if you are happy or sad."

I tried to think about Gale doing what I wanted. She kept looking over her sholder at me.

"What?" I said to the horse but she shook her head.

I guess she culd tell I had no idea what I was doing.

"Come on Bunny." Beth kicked her horse in the side. Gale was already mad at me so I didnt want to kick her. I didnt have to. She bolted after Beths horse. We raced across the open field.

"Wheee!" shouted Beth. "Isnt this fun? Horses are the best. I have my own horse. His name is Lucky. He always knows how I feel. Lucky and I go barrel racing. Do you know barrel racing? You loop around barrels in an arena. Thats where I met Clod. Not many guys do barrel racing but he does and hes really good.

His horse is named Radio—isnt that a weerd name for a horse?"

Good thing Gale was following Beths horse. I culdnt make her do anything. I found myself counting the flies buzzing around her ears. 4 5 6 7. Mean while I went up and down like she was a bouncing castle.

The trail was only wide enuff for 1 horse. Beth led us up a hill and then around some trees. I felt sea sick. 6 7 8 9—unless I was counting the same flies twice. I was going to tell Beth to turn back when she pulled hard on her rains. Her horse stopped short and so did Gale. I fell off. Gale went Nay—laffing again.

Beth pointed left—down the hill. I didnt see anything. Oh wait I did. There was a horse tied up down there.

"Thats a bay," whispered Beth. She slid to the ground and walked both our horses off the path. Then she tied all the rains to a tree and came back. I was on my feet again. We climbed down toward the bay horse.

By the way it was brown. Just so you know. Beth and Clod called it bay but it was a brown horse with a black mane and tail. Whatever. It was tied up near the edge of a big rock. I looked over the edge—and then dropped to my knees and waved at Beth.

"Down there is where the battle is tomorrow," she said. "In that field. Dad told me about it. Back in 1812—"

"Shhh," I said. "And get down."

I grabbed her hand and pulled. Her skin was soft.

There were steps cut into the big rock—steep ones. You culdnt ride to the field down there. You had to walk. Thats what the 1 arm guy had done. His horse was up here near us and he was down there by the white tree. I didnt want him to see us witch is why I told Beth to shhh and get low.

I culdnt see who he was talking to because the tree was in the way. It was a tree you noticed. The only one in the field. Big and old and dead xept for some leaves on one of the branches.

59

A birch tree—theyre the ones with the white bark rite?

The 1 arm guy waved his arm around. The other guy was turned so I culdnt see his face. He nodded like he was agreeing.

"Whos that?" said Beth in a whisper. "He looks like an Indian. Whys the major talking to him?"

"Because theyre friends?"

"He hates Indians. He called me and my dad savages. Remember?"

"Maybe this guy will be on his side tomorrow. I saw guys like him in blue uniforms."

Guys like him. I culdnt say the word Indian and I culdnt think of the rite one. First Nations—but I didnt think of it.

"Doesnt matter," said Beth. "He hates us. War doesnt change who you hate."

I didnt know about that. If these guys were on the same side theyd talk together. Americans used to be our frends xept in hockey—but they were bad guys now. War culd change who you hated all rite.

The guy walked across the battle field away from us.

Battle field. Wow. Seeing the place where the war wuld happen made it seem reeler somehow. I gulped.

"Did you see his face?" Beth whispered.

"No," I said. "Xept side ways for a second. His nose was sharp like a hawk."

Beth shrugged. "That culd be any body. My uncle Jolon has a hawk nose."

"Jolon?"

I was making sure of the name. I knew a Joel and a couple of Johns.

She stared at me. "Yah Jolon," she said. "Hes a grump."

The 1 arm guy started marching back up the steep steps.

"Somethings going on here," said Beth. "Somethings wrong."

"Hes got Spencers phone," I said. "Thats whats wrong."

I went to meet him. Beth followed me talking.

"You go get the horses," I said. "I will be along when I get the phone back."

"I have a better plan," she said. "We shuld sneak after the major and find his tent and then when he isnt looking we shuld—"

"My plan is easier. Im just going to ask him for the phone."

"Well thats—thats—"

Was she going to say stupid? She stomped off without finishing.

He saw me when he was half way up the stairs.

"Hey!" he shouted. "Your the moron right?"

"Thats me," I said. "And your the bully."

Just keeping things clear.

He was puffing. He used his arm to hang onto the railing.

"Do you want me to kick you down these stairs?" he said.

What kind of question was that?

"No," I said.

"Youve got my brothers cell phone," I said. "You found it at the ice cream place. I want it back."

He was up the stairs now. His chest went in and out and in and out. He was sweating.

"Cell phone?" he said. "I dont have one."

"What?" I said.

"There were no cell phones in 1812 you dummy," he said.

He was like Tecumseth. He figured I didnt know anything.

"But this is now," I said. "And you have my brothers cell phone. Give it back."

"I dont have it," he said.

Wow. He was lying. He stood there with his chest going in and out and lying to me like it was a normal thing to do.

"But I saw it," I said. "The phone I mean. I know what it looks like."

"Im a reactor. I dont have a cell phone. Get that thru your thick head."

"Its in your pocket."

"No its not."

So much to take in today. War. A brother in trouble. A girl whose hand was soft. And now grownups lying to me. Not about Santa Claus—a reel lie. *I dont have a cell phone.* It would be like my teacher Miss Nussbaum saying that the capital of Canada is Twix and that whales are insects. Telling us to rite it down because it would be on the test. *Twix Manitoba—capital of Canada. Whales have 6 legs and fly.*

I didnt get the reactor part. The only thing I knew about them was that they were dangerous. Well this guy was dangerous all rite. Mad enough to xplode like a volcano.

I found myself counting the gold buttons on his blue jacket. Its what I do when I dont know what to do. I count things. 11 12 13 14 buttons in two rows.

He was mad but so was I. So we had an argument.

"You have my brothers phone," I said.

"No I dont."

"Yes you do."

"No I dont."

"Yes."

"No."

"Yes."

"No."

"Yes."

It was a pretty silly argument. But we werent laffing.

"Your a moron," he said. "Listen to yourself talk. A real moron."

Name calling now.

"Your a liar," I said. "Listen to the way you talk."

"Theres no body to see us now," he said. "Im going to kick your behind down the steps."

Only he didnt say *behind.* You know what he said.

His leg went back like before you kick a soccer ball. We were facing each other at the top of the steps and he was way bigger than me. If he did kick me Id fall a long way.

He didnt tho. Didnt even try. Because at that moment Tyler stepped out from behind a pine tree.

THERE WERE TREES ALL AROUND US

but Tylers tree was only like 3 feet away. How did he get so close? His sister made a lot of noise when she walked. Tyler was like a secret or a breath. You didnt know he was there.

The 1 arm man said a bad word and pointed at what Tyler was holding.

"Nice tomahawk kid," he said. "Gonna get some scalps tomorrow?"

Tyler smiled. The blade was wide at one end and narrow and sharp at the other. The metal was very bright. A nasty looking weapon.

"Im going now moron," the 1 arm man said to me. "I will deal with you when theres no body around. Count on it."

He walked to where his horse was waiting. A minute later I herd him galloping off. Tyler stuck the tomahawk into his belt. With his hair and fethers and slashes under his eyes he looked perfect—like an old movy. *Dances With Wolves* or something.

I wondered what Tylers movy Native name wuld be. *Talks With Hands* or *Creeps Up On Creeps* maybe.

It wuld take a long time to say.

Imagine if everyone had a movy Native name. Family life wuld be tuff eh? My poor dad calling me and Spencer for dinner would have to shout for 5 minutes.

Come on Doesnt Get Whats Going On But Tries Hard. Dinners ready! he would shout. Thats me. Then hed shout for Spencer. *Come on Knows Lots of Things And Likes Comic Books More Than Sports!*

And it wuld take just as long at bed time.

Maybe Spencer and Bunny are easier. And Tyler.

"So were you there all along?" I asked Tyler. "Did you hear the guy say he didnt have a phone? What a liar eh?"

Tyler shrugged.

The sun shone. The trees russled. I didnt know what to do. If I kept after the 1 arm man hed lie again and maybe kick me down the stairs. Id thot it wuld be easy. Find him and get back my brothers phone. I didnt think hed say no.

He was rite about me—I was a moron.

Tyler moved his hands and shrugged. His face made it clear what he was asking.

"I don't know," I ansered. "What do *you* want to do?"

He smiled and lifted the tomahawk. Holding it by the handle he moved his other hand to tell me to stay back, and then he threw the tomahawk in a strait line. The thing turned over and over and stuck in the trunk of a dead tree.

Crack!

"Good throw," I said. Tyler nodded.

"He can do that all day," said Beth who rode up just then. She was on her horse and leading mine by the rains.

"Old 1 arm galloped off," she said. "He looked mad. Did he give you back the phone?"

I shook my head. "He said he didnt have it."

"But your sure you saw it. So hes lying?"

"Yes."

"We have to do something about that. We need a plan," she said.

She slid off her horse still holding on to both rains—hers and mine. Her face was empty and her eyes were far off. Spencer looks like that when hes thinking. So maybe she was thinking. Good.

I dont know what I look like when Im thinking. I bet I dont look like that. Of course I am not thinking very much.

Tyler came over to pat her. He offered me the tomahawk and looked a question.

"Do I want to throw it? Sure," I said.

A tomahawk is like an ax only cooler. You chop wood with an ax. You scalp guys with a tomahawk. Scalping is gross but it is also cool. Sort of.

Theres a picture of a tomahawk in our book – the part about English words coming from native words. Thats how come I can spell it. Tomahawk. Also skunk and muskrat and husky and tobboggan. Tobaggan. Whatever.

I looked at the dead tree Tyler had stuck with his tomahawk. Culd I do that 2? Tyler clapped his hands to get my attention then made a quick jerking move with his arm—snapping his rist.

"Throw like that? OK," I said. I took a breath and threw.

The tomahawk went right into the ground at my feet.

"Oops."

I tried again. Better. It went all the way to the tree. I tried again. Oops again but in a different way—the tomahawk went strait up and landed on the ground near me. I tried again. This time it hit where I was aiming but didnt stick. Again. Nope. Again. Nope. Again. Nope. Again. Nope.

I was bad at this.

But it was kind of fun. Like darts or other throwing games. Like baseball. I wanted to do better. I gave the tomahawk back to Tyler.

"Show me again," I said.

So he did. It stuck rite in the tree. How did he do that?

"Again," I said. "Slowly. Show me when you let go."

I figured that letting go was key. If you let go late the tomahawk would go into the ground at your feet and if you let go early it would fly into the air.

Tyler threw again—slowly—with an extra rist flip when he let go. It wasnt his best throw but it still hit the tree and stuck for a second. I watched close. He started with his hand over his head and let go when his hand was as hi as his sholder. I thought maybe I culd do it. OK.

"Hey," said Beth.

"Wait," I said.

"Hey hey," said Beth.

Tyler laffed and pointed at the horse. I knew what he was getting at. Hay is what horses eat. It wasnt that good a joke but it kept coming up.

"Yah," I said to him.

"I have a plan for getting your phone," said Beth.

I put down the tomahawk.

TYLER WAS BETTER AT RIDING THAN ME.

He made it look easy—he stepped up into the foot thing and hopped onto Gales back. Boom like that. Then he reached down a hand and pulled me up onto the horse. His arm mussels got tite and bulgy—he was a strong guy. I sat behind him and we rode back to the core al together.

Clod was still there. He helped Beth down. Tyler hopped off. I fell off. Clod walked the horses inside the gate.

Tyler disappeared. When I looked around he was gone. We were half way up on a gentle hill with the river at the bottom and the town at the top. I culd see the bend of the river and the sun flashing on the water. I culd hear the town—the banging and laffing and shouting. Where we were was dusty and grassy with a couple trees.

Where did Tyler go? How did he vanish like that?

Beth asked Clod some questions about the 1 arm man. He had to give his name to borrow a horse so Clod knew stuff about him. He was named Brasher and he wanted the horse for the next day—for the fiting.

"He told me to bring Dancer to his tent early," said Clod. "He gave me a tip before hand."

Clod held out his hand—there was money in it. Green money with a 10 in the corner and a picture of an old guy with whiskers.

"Wow. So you know where Brashers tent is?" asked Beth.

"Sure. Number 3 from the end on the American side of the camp."

"Number 3 eh? Your pretty cool Clod."

"Maybe I am," said Clod. He smiled at Beth. "Maybe I am."

I looked around some more. "Where did Tyler go?" I asked Beth.

She shook her head. "I never know with him," she said.

"Im off duty in a few minutes," said Clod. "Maybe I could use this money to get you an ice cream?"

"No thanks," I said. I was thinking about the way Tyler had stepped from behind the tree when the 1 arm man was talking to me. And he culd vanish when he wanted. Not bad.

Clod frowned at me. "Wasnt talking to you."

"Oh. Good thing I dont want any ice cream then," I said.

Beth smiled. "Maybe Clod wuld get me an ice cream. Bunny—I will see you later."

Good for Tyler. Vanishing was a pretty good power to have I thot.

You ever do that—think witch super power youd like to have? Spencer and I did that sometimes.

Flying was good and being super strong and super fast. I asked Spencer once if being super smart wuld be a good power. He said he didnt think so.

"Youd get good marks in school," he said. "And be on TV quiz shows. But you wuldnt have much fun. Better to be strong—you can punch the bully and pull your friends out of ditches. And your already pretty strong Bun Man."

Making candy out of thin air. We both thot that wuld be a winner super power.

But disappearing…vanishing whenever you wanted. Like being in visible…

Not bad at all.

"Good by now Bunny," said Beth. "Remember my plan. I will see you later."

"Are you going somewhere?"

"No you are."

"Rite," I said. "I have to find Grampa and Spencer." I set off up the hill to the town. It wasnt reely a town. I said that rite? It was more like the mid way at a fair—lots of people and noise. Places to play games and watch things and a path winding thru it.

Where was Spencer? It wuld be nice to see him again. I didnt have his phone but I knew where it was. Beth had a plan to get it back. I wuldnt tell Spencer about her plan in case it didnt work.

When I got to the town I saw more army guys in blue and red uniforms. I wondered about that. In old war movys the uniforms are green to look like the jungle. But there was no jungle here—only a park with trees and a road. I guess if theres no jungle your uniform doesnt have to be green. I saw a guy with a movy camera. He was pointing it at the stage. There was a lot of laffing and clapping. Somebody was wet. That was the game I guess—to turn the bucket over and wet who ever was on the stage.

A troop of fiters stood in an open area. There were 10 of them or maybe 12. They wore red coats and white pants and tall hats. Canadians—they were on our side. They stood in a line while a guy in a wide hat yelled at them. He was the boss telling them what to do.

"I want you to cheer!" he said. "We will win tomorrow and we need to cheer!"

He sounded like Mr Tecumseth or my old soccer coach. *We will win!*

I hoped he was rite.

The red coat guys cheered. "Yay!"

"No!" shouted the guy in the wide hat. "No no no! Not like that!"

Under his wide hat he had hair flowing down to his sholders and when he shook his head his hair flew around. He had big eyes and reel white skin and he didnt look mad even when he was shouting. He looked sad instead. Like he read flower poems and sang songs about being left behind.

I wanted his team to win because theyd be fiting for my country. But I was worryed. He didnt look tuff or sound tuff. Not like the 1 arm American.

"No!" he shouted sadly. "We have to say the rite cheer. Not yay. Shout huzzah!"

"Huzzah," said the red fiters.

"Again."

"Huzzah!"

"Thats better. Shout it tomorrow. Huzzah!"

He smiled now. Even his smile was a bit sad. Like he was pleased but he had a hole in his sock.

The crowd behind me cheered and laffed. There was another game going on. A target was set up against some hay bales—a big piece of paper with a red circle. Like for archery you know? Like that.

The area in front of the target was open. An old lady in shorts and sun glasses held a little ax in the air and waved it around and whooped like she was going to chop some wood. The crowd laffed again. She stepped forward and threw her ax at the target.

Wuld you believe it? The same thing Tyler was teaching me just now. An ax is just a tomahawk right? It turned over once and stuck in the straw.

It was a good throw but missed the target. The crowd went "Ohhhh." The old lady wandered off.

I didnt realize ax throwing was a reel game. Did my school have a team? Id never herd of it.

A guy with suspenders and a big cigar pulled the ax from the target.

"Whos next?" he yelled.

A man near the front put up his hand. He looked like Dr Jin my old doctor—thin and with dark hair and a flat nose. But he had tattoos on his arms and Dr Jin didnt.

"I want to give it a try," he said to the blond woman beside him.

And he sounded like Dr Jin. Did doctors get tattoos? I thot it was only rock stars and gang guys. And pirates.

He threw the ax and missed.

"Tomato!" he shouted.

Witch was Dr Jins favorite swear. He said *tomato* when the tape broke in the middle of my test. "Whats your name?" he asked for the

6th time and I said, "Bunny" for the 6th time and he said, "Your full name" for the 6th time. It was that kind of test. Then he asked me to hold this super scratchy cloth and I dropped it and the tape broke and he said, "Tomato!" I asked him why it was such a bad word. He said it didnt mean tomato in Chinese. "Well it does in English," I said.

The blond woman put her hand up to her mouth. She knew what tomato ment.

I felt a tap on my arm and world around to see who was there. It was Tyler. He smiled and rite away I forgot about Dr Jin.

"How did you DO that?" I asked.

Tyler looked a question.

"How did you sneak up on me? Its like you can find me any where. Is that your super power?"

He laffed without making any noise and punched me.

He pointed at the ax throwing game and then at me. Did I want to?

"I dunno," I said. "But you shuld do it. Youd hit for sure!"

He flapped his hand like good by—like itd be 2 easy.

A BUNCH OF THINGS
HAPPENED THEN.

Lets see if I can get them in order.

1) The 1 arm guy showed up beside the stage. He had a sord in his hand. A reel sord—not one made of card bord. He was yelling at some other guys in blue. They yelled back and moved their guns around in their hands. This way that way. Pointing up and then side ways and then ready to fire. They looked like a reel army—way tuffer than the sad poetry guy and his huzzah troops. I worried about the fite tomorrow. How culd we win against these Americans?

Tyler saw them 2. He made a face.

"Hes a reactor," I said—meaning he was dangerous. A bomb. Tyler nodded like he knew that. So that was 1 thing.

2) I saw Grampa. He was down the street from the stage near the log cabin. He had changed hats. Now he was wearing his flat black one instead of the one with the hooks on it. He looked more like Grampa now. He went over to the old lady sitting in front of the log cabin and gave a little bow— like a penguin you know? That was even weerder. Then he grabbed her hand! That was weerdest of all. Old people holding hands was totally weerd. Back home Dad wuld sneak up on Mom and kiss her and she wuld roll her eyes. That was a bit weerd. And they were younger than Grampa and his girl frend. Even writing that down is weerd. Grampas girl frend.

At first I was going to run over and tell him about the war coming up the next day so we culd all leave. But when I saw him holding the old ladys hand I culdnt move.

3) I saw Beth and Clod. They stood near the stage eating ice cream cones and smiling at each other.

4) I got mad.

This wasnt in order. My getting mad didnt happen all at once. I must of been getting mad for a wile.

I dont know why. But I did. It was weerd. I had a hole lot of stuff bubbling up inside me and it all came out—like when Dad makes pasta and the pot is boiling with the lid on. My pot of stuff had a lot in it. The war the next day. The 1 arm bully lying about Spencers phone. And something else. I didnt know what it was. I didnt like Beth eating Clods ice cream and I didnt like Grampa holding the old ladys hand. It didnt make any sense but then your feelings dont always make sense. It was—I dont know—something. It made me so hot I boiled over.

I stomped over to the ice creamers. Stomp stomp stomp. 21 22 23 stomps.

"Hi," I said to Beth. Not to Clod.

"Hi Bunny," said Beth. "Do you like butter-scotch ice cream? The place by the park gates has the best. Clod got me some. Its reely good. I was going to get chocolate like I usually do. And then I saw a tub with a fat gooey line of butterscotch running thru the golden yellow ice cream and it looked so good I had to try it. Sometimes butter-scotch is 2 sweet you know? So sweet it makes your mouth sore. But not this kind—its sweet but not 2 sweet. You can have some of mine if you want."

Clod was smiling to himself while Beth was talking. I wanted to punch him.

"Butterscotch tastes like farts," I said loud.

Yah I know. Not very nice. Or funny. I shuld of done better than that.

Beth laffed a little laff. Clod didnt. He said, "What?"

I ran off. I didnt think where I was going— just ran. I ended up at the front of the crowd near the guy holding the ax and yelling for a volun-teer. I was in the front row. The target was rite over there.

I didnt see the circles tho. I saw Beth and Clod eating ice cream. Their heads were together right in the middle of the target. I grabbed the ax and threw hard. I flicked my rist as I let go. The ax hit right in the middle of Clods face—I mean rite in the middle of the target.

"Tomato!" I yelled.

And ran back through the cheering laffing crowd.

I KEPT RUNNING.

The picture of Clod with the ax in his head made me feel better. But I didnt get it. Why did I want to ax him? Because he ate ice cream? I kept running. My heart felt like it was going to come thru my ribs.

Thump.

Thump.

Thump.

I came to a table with pistols on it. A guy in a red coat held one in his hand. It was the biggest thing. Like a chain saw. He stuck something down the barrel of the gun. I culdnt tell if he was cleaning it or loading it. People took pictures.

I thot about shooting Clod with one of the pistols—a bad idea even for me.

Dont shoot Clod.

Thats what I thot. I ran on trying not to think about shooting Clod.

Thump.

Dont shoot Clod.

Thump.

Dont shoot Clod.

Thump.

I started counting the thumps. I got up to 173. That was 173 times I didnt shoot Clod. Then I lost count and started again. This time I got to 57 before I lost count. I was near the end of the town with woods on both sides. People all around me but no body very close. Fiters in blue uniforms and red. People in normal clothes. The sun was behind me and my shadow was in front. The hill going down to the stream on my rite and the road leading out of the park to my left.

I ran along the road out of the park to the ice cream place.

Thump.

Thump.

The ice cream place was where Spencer left his phone. And it was where Clod and Beth went to get the butterscotch. As soon as I thot about that I wanted to shoot Clod all over again.

I stopped when a giant black bird flew at me. It had shiny feathers and a harsh sound like an old man coffing. *Hork hork.* A crow only bigger. A super crow. I ducked and the big black bird flew past my head.

Hork.

Shoot Clod.

Shoot Clod now.

Hork.

I stood in the middle of the road with my heart thumping and sweat pouring off my forehead like a waterfall. What was wrong with me? Why was I so upset? So angry? So—I dont know. So Clod got Beth some ice cream—so what?

Beth.

She was why. When I thot about her my heart thumped louder than ever. Like a dog pounding its tail on the ground.

Somebody was behind me. I culd hear them breathing. I turned slowly. I didnt know what Id do if it was Clod. But it wasnt.

It was Tyler.

He must of followed me. I didnt know—he moved quiet. Now his bare chest went up and down as he breathed. His ribs stretched in and out. His eyes were on me. He looked me a question.

I shrugged.

"I dont know," I said. "I dont know why I ran away."

He moved his hand like—go on.

"Well—I was thinking about Clod and Beth eating ice cream and—and then I started running," I said. "Thats all."

He nodded and smiled like—Ah ha.

"What?" I said. "What do you think? Do you think I like Beth?"

He nodded. Smiled. Kept smiling.

"Shut up," I said.

He culdnt stop smiling.

"Im not," I said. "I mean I dont." Now I was smiling myself.

He held up his hands like he was saying—OK enuff. New topic.

He pointed back toward the stage. He pulled out his tomahawk and made like he was throwing it. He pointed at me and clapped like—way to go.

"Yah," I said. "I hit the target."

We walked back into the park. I felt better but still kind of—I dont know. Upset. Angry. Something. I was glad Tyler was beside me. Every now and then Id sneak a look over to make sure he was still there—he culd vanish so fast. Hed look back at me and smile. That made me feel better.

* * *

People were lined up next to a big fire pit. A woman in a long dress cut pieces of meat off an animal who was lying down without a head. Sorry—that sounds weerd. The animal was dead and the lady was cooking it on the fire. There was a stick running thru it and the woman turned the stick so different parts of the animal wuld cook.

It smelled so smoky and good that that I totally forgot about feeling upset.

Tyler pointed at the line up of people and looked a question at me.

"Id love to have some," I said. "But I dont have any money."

Tyler shook his head. He held out a hand like to buy something and then slapped himself. Shook his head again. Then he pointed at the roasting animal bar bq. And held out his hands like—help yourself.

"Free?" I said. "The food is free?"

He nodded and smiled.

"Oh. Well then. Sure," I said. "Lets get some."

The meat was black and tasted like smoke. You culd pick it up and eat it out of your hand

and then throw the bones in the fire when you were done. It was great.

I kept my eyes open for Spencer. I missed him. I wanted to tell him I was hoping to get back his phone and have him say hello to Tyler. I knew theyd like each other—it wuldnt bother Spencer that Tyler didnt talk. Spencer didnt mind stuff like that.

The short guy with the little hat walked by. He scratched on his fiddle. It sounded like the farmer in the dell.

A TV woman came by with a camera on her sholder. She was young—more like a kid. This wasnt the same one I saw before with the flip flops. She pointed the camera at the fiddler. Then at the animal turning on the fire. Then she came to our table and filmed Tyler for a bit.

"Your perfect," she said. "Just keep eating. Don't talk," she said.

Tyler nodded. He wasnt going to say anything no matter what she asked him.

It was so quiet I heard a woman in the distance shouting, "WHAT WAS THAT?"

The camera woman frowned.

Not seeing Beth and Clod made me pleased and sad at the same time. Weerd eh? I wanted to see Beth. Itd be nice to see her even if she was with him. But I also didnt want to see her with him.

Yeesh.

I went back to the meat.

"SPEAK UP! I DIDNT HEAR YOU!" shouted the lady in the distance.

People who were eating their dinners near by saw the TV girl filming us and came over to take their own pictures. Well not me—no body wanted me. But Tyler got a lot of attention. They asked him stuff but of course he didnt say anything. One guy in a beerd and a checkered shirt watched for a bit and then came over to say how much he admired Tylers silence.

"Your the wise one," said this guy. His dark beerd was thin and so was he. His sleeves were rolled up. His jeans were so tight you culd see his knee bones thru them. He wore glasses like Harry Potter. He was a serious guy. Intents you know?

"Way to stay in side yourself man," he said to Tyler. "Dont talk. Dont say anything. Your people have the wisdom of the earth and the sky on your side. You carry it with you. I admire that. Im like you inside. My body is from North York but my soul is First Nations. I love nature. I wish this country looked the way it did before selfish whites came along and stole everything. Your silence is testimony man. I like it a lot. Its a deep calm silence. Save your fury for the fite tomorrow."

The guy turned to stare at me.

"I dont have much wisdom," I said.

He frowned but didnt look away from me. Still pretty intents.

"Is there sauce on my cheek?" I asked. "Is that why your staring?"

Now he walked away. Tyler punched me on the sholder.

I heard that loud voice again. The one from the old lady who culdnt hear.

"DAVID MCLEAN!" she said. "I'M TALKING TO YOU!"

Oops!

I stood up.

"David McLean is my grampa," I said to Tyler. "I forgot all about him."

There was so much to think about in the park that afternoon that my brain was full. This happens to me a lot. I find out something new and get interested in it and then I keep thinking about it or doing it and forget about whatever I was supposed to remember. Even if that was an important thing—like checking in with Grampa.

Dr Jin wanted me to work on this. I didnt get it. How can you PRACTICE remembering? Your brain is not a trumpet. You cant sit down every day and remember for an hour. How wuld you know you were doing it rite? And what if you forgot 1 day? Or 2 days? Youd have to remember to remember.

Maybe I shuld just write stuff down. Xept Id probly lose the paper I wrote on.

"Ive got to go," I said to Tyler. "My grampa told me to check in at dinner time. I will see you later."

He made a sine like he was talking on the phone.

"Right," I said. "Beths plan to get Spencers phone back. That starts later."

He nodded.

"DAVID MCLEAN HOW DARE YOU!"

The loud voice was coming from not very far away.

I put down my empty glass of lemon ade.

Tyler clapped his hands once. Pointed to his chin.

"Oh thanks," I said.

I wiped. And went to find my grampa.

HE WAS IN FRONT OF THE LOG CABIN.

There was a bench and he was sitting on it. Beside him was the old lady he was holding hands with before. His girl frend.

They werent holding hands now. The lady was glaring at Grampa and he was looking away. Wow. Grampa was in trouble.

This was weerd. I didnt know he culd get in trouble. He was Moms dad. Hed been every where in the world. We all did what he told us to do—even Mom. How culd he be in trouble?

He was trying to xplain to the lady but she wasnt getting it.

"I didn't—"

"YOU SAID THEY WERE OVER POWERING," she said.

"No," he said. "No I didnt."

"HOW DARE YOU! MY FEET ARE NOT OVERPOWERING. NOT AT ALL."

"I didnt say—"

"I WEAR SIZE 6. THATS NORMAL SIZE. NOT OVERPOWERING."

She had a voice like a siren on a fire truck. She didnt look like she was shouting. This was natural talking for her. Every body near by culd hear—the same way every body can hear a siren. People all down the way were looking at her and Grampa.

"Heat!" he said in a loud voice. "The HEAT is overpowering."

"Oh," she said.

"Your feet are fine," he said. "Your feet are lovely."

Wow. This did not sound like Grampa.

"Oh Poochy," she said again. "YOU ARE A DEVIL," she said.

I walked up to the table. Slowly.

"Hi," I said to him.

"Oh. Uh hello Bernard." Grampa checked his watch. "Right on time. Humph," he said.

"Good," I said.

I nodded at the lady. "Hi," I said.

"Irene this is my grandson Bernard," said Grampa. "Bernard this is my frend Mrs Steel."

She stood up and we shook hands. "CALL ME IRENE," she said.

"Im Bunny," I said.

"THATS RIGHT," she said with a big smile. "YOU ARE FUNNY."

Even when she wasnt mad she talked like a siren. Her lungs were great.

"Bunny," I said.

"HA-HA HA-HA," she said. Her laff was like a siren 2—one of those sirens on English TV that go *doo-dot doo-dot.* Come to think of it she talked like she was on English TV. And dressed like it 2. She wore an old timey hat that looked like a pot holder.

And she called Grampa Poochy. Wait til I told Spencer. I culdnt see how big her feet were because her dress went down over her shoes.

"What have you been up to this afternoon Bernard?" said Grampa.

"I went horse back riding," I said.

I wasnt going to say anything about Spencers cell phone.

Mrs Steele—Irene—leaned forward to listen.

"WHATS YOUR NAME?" she asked me.

"His name is Bernard," said Grampa loudly.

Irene's face cleared. "THAT XPLAINS IT," she said.

She didnt say what it xplaned.

"DID YOU SAY YOU WERE ON A HORSE BERNARD?"

"YES," I said loud so she culd hear me.

Grampa smiled. "Its good to try new sports," he told me.

"WHAT KIND OF HORSE?" Irene asked. I didnt know what she ment. I didnt know there were different kinds. A horse was a horse.

They were big animals with 4 legs and long noses. And manes. People rode them. They ate hay.

"Her name is Gale," I said.

The sun was lower down in the sky so the shadows were longer. The park was as busy as ever. People sold candles and made horse shoes. Other people walked up and down the wood chip main road and took pictures. The most popular tables were the ones with guns and sords and guys in uniform.

Lots of pictures at these tables.

I wondered.

A bang sounded from down the way. I was used to the noise by now—it had been going on all afternoon.

"Thats a gun," I said to Grampa.

"It is," he said. "A musket."

"A reel one," I said. "A reel gun."

He nodded. How culd he be so calm about it?

"You know theres a war tomorrow," I said. "Us and the Americans. Do you know that?"

"Its why we came," he said. "Remember I said there wuld be a surprise?"

"A war?" I said. "Thats the surprise?"

He nodded.

"But wars are terrible—right? Dad says so."

Grampa laffed. And I remembered that hed been in wars before. Big ones. World wars. This fite in the park wuldnt seem that terrible to him.

Thats why he was so calm.

"What if we lose?" I said. "What then?"

Wuld we become American? And what wuld that mean—being American?

If I was American Id have a different anthem. O say can you see. I didnt know it all but I knew that part. No more standing on gard. If I was American Id have a president. My capital city wuld be Washington. Id have green money.

Not much else tho eh? Id talk the same tho I mite have a funny axent. But about the same. Id watch the same TV shows and movys. Learn the same math in school. Live with my family. Pretty much like now.

But what if Spencer got hurt in the fite tomorrow? Or Grampa? Or me? What if one of us lost an arm like that Major Brasher? Or if we died? Then things wuld change a lot. Losing a war was bad. But not as bad as getting killed. Id still be me even if we lost the war. I didnt want to be American. But I reely didnt want to be dead.

Huh. So wars werent about losing your anthem or your money or your capital city. You culd lose you.

Dad was rite. Wars were terrible.

Then I thot that if I culd think all this then why culdnt every body else? Im not the smartest guy around. That chicken with the cups? I bet it wuld get that wars were bad.

"Dont worry Bernard," Grampa said. "We wont lose. General Brock is a good fiter."

"And Mr Tecumseth," I said.

"Tecumseth? Yes. He was a great general. Maybe the best in the hole war."

I was going to tell Grampa how I met the great general but just then 2 guys came up to stare at the big wooden wheel that was standing up on a bench near where we were. Irene went over to them.

"THIS IS A REEL SPINNING WHEEL," she began.

A GUY TOOK PICTURES OF THE CHAIN SAW SIZE PISTOLS.

He was facing away so I saw his back pack. It had an American flag on it. He was the enemy. And he was taking pictures of our stuff. I thot about that.

"Grampa do you know anything about spying?" I asked.

"What do you mean Bernard?" He sounded sharp like a knife.

"That guy with the camera," I said. Pointing. "He culd be a spy. If he sends his pictures to America theyll know about our weapons."

People had been taking pictures all day long.

Grampa relaxed. He told me not to worry.

"Hes no more a spy than YOU are Bernard," he said.

When Irene came back he told her. It took a while but she finally understood.

"SPYING?" she said to me. "YOU ASKED DAVID MCLEAN ABOUT SPYING? THATS PRICELESS, DEAR BOY. HA-HA HA-HA."

Grampa squeezed her hand.

He asked if I was hungry. Did I want to have dinner with him and Irene? There was going to be stew and other stuff for every body in the camp. I didnt want to eat with them because old people holding hands was weerd. But I didnt want to say no because that wuld be rude.

"Im ok now—I already ate something," I said. Then I asked where Spencer was.

"Dont you know Bernard?" said Grampa. "He said he was going to get you."

Oh oh. Shuld I know where Spencer was? Was I in trouble? Was he? I didnt know what to say.

"Uhhhh," I said.

One of the good things about being me is that nobody expects me to sound smart. I get away with way more than Spencer. When I said *uhhh* Grampa just nodded.

"SPENCER IS A DARLING. IM GLAD HE AND TRACEY ARE GETTING ALONG," said Irene.

Suddenly I thot of Beth. I saw her face and hair and fether. I saw her smile and her eyes and her hands holding the rains. I heard her voice. Why? Why would Spencer and Tracey getting along make me think of Beth? But thats what happened.

"Uhhh," I said again.

I didnt want to stay around.

"You know where our tents are Bernard. I want you back there for bed time. Remember to stay in bounds. Dont cross the road."

"Yes Grampa," I said.

"And say good nite when you get to your tent. Can I trust you?"

"I will do my best," I said. "Have a nice dinner."

I dashed off after the American with the back pack and the camera. I wanted to see what he was up to. Grampa was sure he wasnt a spy but what did Grampa know about spying?

(Thats what I thot about Grampa back then. I know a bit more now.)

I followed the American. Like a detective you know? He moved along slow and creaky and took pictures of weapons. I stayed back and watched him. I was in visible. He never knew I was there. I tracked him down to the place with the horses— the core al. There werent as many people around witch made following tuff. After a while it was just me and the guy. There was nothing to hide behind. He patted a horse on the nose then turned and looked at me.

"Say! You again," he said.

Oops.

"Again?" I said.

"I recognize that shirt. Youve been behind me for a while."

He pointed.

"Bread was a great band," he said. "I remember them from when I was your age. Im a fat old man now but I was young and groovy once."

Maybe I wasnt quite as in visible as I thot.

"Say! Let me take a picture," he said.

"A picture—"

"Of you and your shirt. So I can show every body back home."

"Your from America," I said.

"You bet. Buffalo born and proud of it! Say! Dont move."

So I stood there and let him take a picture. He shook my hand and told me his name was Elmer. Like the glue he said. I told him my name. He said he was glad to meet me. Then he took pictures of the horses and started back up the hill.

"You coming Bunny?" he asked.

"I think I will stay here," I said.

"OK. See you tomorrow in the battle."

So was he a spy? I didnt know. He was an enemy and seemed nice. That's all I knew. He had my picture and knew my name.

I must of been the worst detective ever.

*   *   *

The sine on the core al said it was closed. Horses ate grass and trotted around. Maybe Gale was there and maybe not. I culdnt tell. It was getting darker. Not much but a bit. I was at the bottom of the hill looking up. The sun was below the trees above me. The air was cooler. It smelled like horse poop. But thats not a terrible smell.

I leaned my back on the top of the fence and wondered where every body was. Clod was ether home for the nite or with Beth. Spencer was ether looking for me or with Tracey. Grampa and Irene were on their way to dinner.

I felt a tap on my sholder from behind. It came from inside the fence. The only one I culd think of in there was Gale and she wuldnt tap me on the sholder. I turned and there was Tyler with his white smile.

How did he do that?

"Were you here all along?" I asked. "Looking like a horse?"

He shook his head and made walking moves with his fingers.

"You were following me?"

He nodded.

"Down the hill? From up top?"

He nodded again.

"I was following that fat American guy but he saw me. Do you think he saw you?"

Tyler shook his head.

"Wow. You are good," I said.

NOTHING IMPORTANT HAPPENED UNTIL LATE AT NITE.

Somebody shook me and woke me up. The tent was dark. I culdnt see who it was. Spencer? Then a hand went over my mouth.

No wait. Some stuff happened before that. Sorry. I forgot about Laura Secord and the farb guy. I should tell about that first.

* * *

We hung out—Tyler and me. The sun went down. We looked at some stars with his telescope and hit some trees with his tomahawk.

114

Some American soldiers were playing cards in front of a big tent. We hid behind the next tent and watched them for a while. We didnt find anything out. Then a tall guy with red whiskers came out of the woods and glared at them.

"You guys are eating chips!" he yelled. "Drinking beer out of bottles. That is farb!"

"Hi Luther," said the dealer.

Luther didnt say hi back. He pointed at one of the players.

"Just what are you wearing Hadley?" he shouted. His finger shook—thats how upset he was.

Hadley had on tight white uniform pants and a t shirt. He looked down at himself and held out his hands like he was saying—What?

"That is a t shirt!" said Luther. "A tie die t shirt! Do you think this is the summer of love? This is 1812! Farb Hadley! Farb!"

No one asked what he ment. They all knew.

Luthers pointing finger was long and thin and dirty. Like him. There were sticks and mud hanging off him. His boots were ragged. He looked like a hobo in a uniform. His red whiskers were amazing. Like a beerd growing side ways out of his cheeks.

"Farb?" I whispered to Tyler. He made a gagging face.

"Like sick? Bad? Lame?"

He nodded.

Luther was as angry as a kettle. He hissed and spit and shook. He grabbed the table and jerked it up and over. The players shouted and got out of the way. The cards went flying.

Luther stomped away shouting "farb" over and over. "Farb farb farb."

"He wrecked their game," I said.

Tyler nodded.

"If you ask me Luther is farb."

Tyler nodded again.

A noise came from the other side of the tent we were hiding behind. A cry of "Oh no" and the tent fell down. And there was Beth. She looked embarrassed.

"Hi," she said. She held a piece of metal.

"I bumped the pole," she said.

Tyler was laffing to himself. He went round and helped his sister put up the tent again. I tried not to think about Clod. I was happy to see Beth again tho.

The card players stared at us.

"Sorry," Beth called to them. "That was me. Your tents OK now."

The three of us walked off together. Beth was in the middle.

"I reely shuld learn to track better," she said. "Im a disgrace—probably the noisiest Indian in the world. Eh Tyler?"

Tyler nodded.

"Are you feeling better Bunny?" she asked me.

"Better than what?"

"Better than you were before. You seemed mad."

"No I wasnt," I said. "I wasnt mad at all. Not at all."

"You sure?"

"Yes!"

"Gee now you sound mad all over again."

"Im not," I said. "And you shut up Tyler!"

You culdnt hear any thing but he was laffing all right.

We went back to their tent. It was on the other side of the camp from ours. There was a fire in front of it. Mr Tecumseth was there with 3 other guys. 2 of them had fethers in their hair and wore red uniforms like Mr Tecumseths. The other one had a blanket rapped around him and pulled up so I didnt see his face. Mr Tecumseth nodded when he saw us. Beth and Tyler sat down on a log on the other side of the fire. Tyler pulled me down so I was sitting with them. Mr Tecumseth told the guys who I was. He remembered my name.

"Hi," I said.

They nodded. One of them said something. Mr Tecumseth said something else. Then they all started talking together.

They werent speaking English. Or French—I dont know much French but I know some and it didnt sound like this. An other language then.

Tyler and Beth nodded like they understood. I guess it was their language.

I nodded along. Pretending I knew. I did that in French class.

Jam a pell. 2 a pell. Eel a pell.

I nodded along with the teacher even tho I didnt know what kind of jam she was talking about or why an eel wuld need some.

The sun was down but there was still some lite in the sky. The guys were talking and nodding. I watched Beth and Tyler and nodded whenever they did.

Then I herd a word I knew. I herd it again. *Secord.* I listened hard and herd another word. *Laura.*

Now I knew what they were talking about.

Candy.

Mom always got Laura Secord candy on her birthday. I culd see the box—dark red with gold writing and a picture of a girl looking side ways. Tasty stuff. No wonder every body here was nodding.

Did they bring out any candy? No. They just talked about it. Mr Tecumseth took a round thing out of his pocket and held it up to the fire. Beth nudged me.

"Nice watch eh?" she whispered.

I didnt know what she ment.

"What time is it Dad?" she asked in English.

"After 11," he said.

The thing was a clock. A pocket clock! I wuld of said something but I didnt have time. If it was 11 I was late.

I stood up and said I had to go. Beth and Tyler stood up with me.

"By," I said to every body. "Good luck tomorrow."

Mr Tecumseth waved calmly. The others nodded.

We walked past the guy in the blanket.

"Excuse me Uncle Jolon," said Beth.

I saw him side ways in the fire light. Big nose and chin. He grunted something and then I forgot about him because Beth tripped and fell rite into me and I was holding her.

"Stop pushing," she said to Tyler who was behind her.

He waved his hands.

"What do you mean?" she said to him. He waved some more.

"He—uh—wants you to walk with me back to my camp," I said.

"What?" She turned around. Tyler was nodding.

I blushed. I culd feel it. It was dark so no body saw.

Beth frowned at me. "You know what Tyler means better than I do," she said. "Youve only known him a day. How come your so smart?"

Tyler pointed at me and then at Beth.

"I can find my own way. I will see you later," I said to both of them. And ran.

WHERE DOES TIME GO?

I mean reely. Time was there all evening. I culd feel it passing slowly as I watched the card players and listened to the talk about candy. And now time was gone. Time had run out. I was late. Is there a hole time falls into? Does time play hide and seek? Where does it go?

I headed for our camp site—wherever that was. I didnt know. I was afraid it wuld take a long time but I found the paved road rite away and followed it around to our camp. The moon was up so I culd see OK. And there were camp fires. People near by played music and sang about somebody coming round the mountain when she came.

Our 2 tents were side by side. I walked past Grampas tent and crawled into the other and rite off there was a problem—somebody was in my sleeping bag.

Was it the wrong tent? No because there was Spencer. I culd see his face. His glasses were off but it was him all rite. So who was in my sleeping bag? I checked—it wasnt any body. It was my clothes. Somebody had stuffed them in the bag.

Weerd.

I bundled the clothes to make a pillow and found my tooth brush and used it—sort of. I slid off my shorts and got into my bag. Then I remembered Grampa telling me to make sure to say good nite.

I sat up and cleared my throat.

"Nite Grampa," I said into the dark. Well the pretty dark. His tent was close enuff for him to hear me if he was awake.

Nothing.

So I said it louder.

"Nite Grampa."

Spencer must of herd me. He mumbled something. Was he awake?

"Nite Spencer," I said.

He turned over. He was breathing deep. He was asleep the hole time.

"Weve already done this Bernard," said Grampa from his tent. His voice sounded clear as a bell. A grumpy bell.

"We have?" I said.

"Every body has said good nite to every body else. Now go to sleep."

So I did. I lay down with my clothes for a pillow and dreamed about riding. In my dream I wore a cowboy hat and carried an ax and galloped across the desert on Gale the horse. She looked over her sholder and said, *Hey.*

Thats what you eat, I said. She laffed. Then she asked how come I was so smart. I patted her. *Your feet are lovely*, I said in my dream.

And then somebody shook me and woke me up. The tent was still dark. I culdnt see who it was. Spencer? A hand went over my mouth. Oh yah. I remembered now. This was Tyler. It was almost dawn. He and Beth and I were on our way to get Spencers phone back. This was her plan.

I thot about waking Spencer and decided no. Hed be so impressed when I gave him his phone. *Here you go*, Id say and hed say, *Wow*.

I nodded my head and Tyler took his hand off my mouth. I got into my shorts and followed him out the tent door. We jogged thru the sleeping camp. It was so late it was early. The sun wasnt up but there was a faint hint of lite at the bottom of the sky. There was some bird talk going on. They were waking up in the dark.

Tyler knew where he was going. We went down a hill and passed thru a line of small tents in the woods. Some of the tents had fire places in front and some had clothes lines strung up between trees. I saw more than one blue uniform hanging up.

Beth was waiting for us with a small plastic bucket witch she gave to Tyler. She put her finger to her mouth.

"Thats his tent over there," she whispered to me. "With the flag on it."

An American flag but it looked wrong—not enuff stars and stripes.

I remembered Beths plan to scare the 1 arm man out of his tent.

"What kind of animal did you bring?" I asked her. I was looking for a cage.

"Shhh."

She shook her head and pointed at Tyler who was standing a part from us with his hands a bit out from his sides. It was still dark.

"What?" I whispered.

"Tyler is amazing," she whispered. "Watch."

She pulled me away. At this distance I culdnt see Tylers black hair. I culdnt see his skin very well. I culd just make out his lether pants—the ones with the frinj. And the plastic bucket in one hand. He stood there without moving. I mean without moving a mussel. Without breathing it looked like. He stood and stood and stood and stood. And stood some more. I moved more watching him than he did standing in front of the 1 arm mans tent.

A bird flew over him. Big gray one with a sad voice.

He stood some more.

A fast little bird flew around and around him. And around him. And around. Like water going down a drain. Beth grabbed my arm. I culd feel her nails. Huh. She stared at her brother. Biting her lip. The little bird flew in smaller circles getting closer and closer to Tyler. It landed on his arm and took off and landed again next time around. It kept coming back.

The day was getting liter. The big gray bird perched on Tylers head and sounded sad.

And then—

Nothing. Tyler stood there like a statue. Until the little bird landed one more time on his arm and he moved his other hand like a—

like a—rattle snake or mouse trap. Snap. And plopped the plastic bucket over the little bird and covered the top of the bucket with his other hand.

He turned. I saw his teeth clearly. He was smiling.

Beth was clapping without making noise. I did it as well because—well because what Tyler had done was awe some.

"That's not a bird in the bucket is it?" I said to her.

"Nope. Get ready now."

Tyler walked over to the 1 arm mans tent and opened the flap and put the bucket up to the opening. He shook the bucket and then stepped away. The animal was inside the tent now.

I went up to the tent flap and crouched down. Gave Tyler an other silent clap. He nodded. Smiled.

Beth screamed.

EVER WOKEN UP WITH A BAT IN YOUR ROOM?

I have. This weerd zig zag flying thing squeaking so hi I culd hardly hear it. Theres a tree outside my bedroom at home and bats live in the tree and fly into my room if I leave my window open the wrong way witch I sometimes do.

First time this happened to me I turned on the lite and froze. I was surprised. And scared. The bat didnt fly strait. I didnt know where itd go next. I sat there watching it zig zag around. It never bumped into me or my chair or my shelf or the wall or anything. Ever. It looked like it wuld and then it zigged or zagged out of the way.

I counted like I do when Im scared. I counted the times it flew around. After about 50 times it was pretty cool. Then after 200 times I got tired and I wasnt scared any more and I went back to sleep. In the morning the bat was hanging on my shelf. I put on gloves and took it outside.

This was a few years ago. Ive had a few more bats in my room since then. Or maybe the same one over and over again—its hard to tell with bats.

* * *

Beth knew Tyler culd bring animals to him in some weerd way. Her plan was for him to put an animal in the 1 arm mans tent to scare him out so I culd look for Spencers phone.

"Are you afraid of animals?" she asked me when she was xplaning her plan.

"Like lions?" I said. "Like sharks and grizzlys?"

"Like squirrels or birds. Are you afraid to be in a tent with a bird?"

"No," I said.

"Can you find stuff that is lost?"

Funny she shuld ask that. There is so much that I am not good at. But I can find things. Mom says I am the best she knows at finding things. I have found her keys 38 or 39 times.

"Yes," I said.

"Then my plan can work," said Beth.

Tyler made a fluttery motion with his hands at his neck.

"What about bats?" Beth asked. "Are you afraid of bats? Lots of people are."

"No," I said.

Now there was a bat in the 1 arm mans tent. And he was awake thanks to Beth screaming outside. A lite went on in there. A flash lite it looked like. I saw shadows thru the tent wall. Zig zags and waving arms. Sorry—waving arm. I herd shouting. The 1 arm man said a bad word and then another one and then a bunch in a row. He pored out of the tent waving his hands. Hand.

"Help!" he shouted. And then, "A bat," he shouted. "Is it in my hair? Is it? Is it?"

Lites came on in other tents. People were calling out wanting to know what was going on. And wanting the noise to stop.

Beth grabbed the 1 arm guy.

"Let me help," she said.

She held her jacket in one hand. Now she put it over his head.

"Hang on," she said. "I'll help you. Wait— whats that? Oh dear. Dont move. Is that a bat? Oh dear. Don't move. Don't move."

I was already inside the tent.

It was almost day time and the flash lite was still on. What Im saying is that I culd see inside the tent. Sleeping bag all bunched up. Big back pack. And clothes from yesterday.

Where was Spencers phone? Where where where where where? In the 1 arm mans shoe? No. Under his sleeping bag? No. In the tent pocket? No. I looked fast.

I was aware of 2 things. First thing—time. Tick tick tick. The 1 arm man culd come back any second. Like now. Or now. Or now. I counted under my breath.

Second thing—the bat. It was not in the mans hair. Beth was lying. It was still in the tent. I wasnt scared but it was distracting.

The 1 arm mans clothes from yesterday were on the floor. I checked thru them. Jacket? No. Shirt.

And I was aware of a third thing. This was stealing. I was in a strangers tent going thru his stuff. Thats not good. Ive been to Sunday school. I know about Moses and the 10 things you arent supposed to do. Stealing is one of them.

But the 1 arm man stole first. He stole Spencers phone and I was stealing it back. That was OK rite? Rite?

I know what you are thinking—2 wrongs dont make a rite. Well you are wrong. If somebody pushes you down you push them back. If somebody jumps on your frend you jump on them. If they are bigger than you—well you jump anyway. Or get help and then jump.

I thot about it and decided I was OK with stealing from this guy. Plus he said bad things about Beth and Tyler and Mr Tecumseth. I didnt think very long. Time was ticking. The 1 arm man culd come back now. Or now.

Shirt again to make sure. Pants?

Or now. Or now. There was the bat again. I waved it away.

What about pants?

Yes.

His pants were white. The brite yellow phone was in the front pocket.

"Look out! Bunny! Look out!"

Beths voice came from rite outside.

The front flap of the tent was open. I bumped into the 1 arm man as I ran out. He went down and I kept going.

I dont know what happened to the little bat. I never saw it again.

I looked back when I got across the open part of the camp site. The 1 arm man was on the ground staring at me. It was lite enough to see that he wore 1 piece underwear with buttons like in a cartoon. And that he was mad.

"You!" he shouted at me.

Not much you can say to that. I mean it was me all rite.

He stood up and waved his arm.

"Stop!" he shouted. "Stop thief!"

I didnt know people reely said that. I didnt stop.

We were running thru woods. The sun was up. Bitty dots of lite sprinkled thru the leaves like sugar on corn flakes. Beth was with me. Her legs were shorter than mine but we ran the same speed.

"That was close," she said. "Wasnt it?"

I nodded.

"I tried to pull him away before he culd get you. Tyler was behind the tent. I think he was going to take down the tent if the 1 arm went in—and then get you out somehow. Tylers a strange one eh? You shuld know Bunny. You always seem to get what hes saying. I guess your a strange one yourself."

I wondered where Tyler was now. I wasnt worryed about him. Tyler wasnt somebody you worryed about.

We ran some more.

"So did you get it?" she asked. "Im dying to know. Was it there? Did you find it? Did you get your brothers phone?"

I showed it to her.

"Woo hoo!" she said. "You reely ARE good at finding things!"

She reached over and grabbed my hand and squeezed.

I thanked her for her plan.

"I culdnt of found the phone without you," I said. "And Tyler."

We were running past a big camp site. American flags flew from 2 of the tents. Enemy tents. Thats rite—the battle was today.

"I hate that 1 arm guy," said Beth. "And you stood up to him at Dads table when he was calling you names. Of course I wanted to help you. And the idea came to me when we were riding."

She kicked a stone by axident and it banged against a pot. She stumbled and almost fell. We were still holding hands. I pulled her up rite. She fell against me insted of onto the ground.

"Oops," she said.

"Thats OK," I said.

We turned rite and slowed down. We were both breathing hard. I didnt know how she culd talk so much while she ran.

"Are you worryed about helping me?" I said. "The 1 arm guy saw you. He culd tell your dad on you."

She shook her head. "What wuld he say—that we are better stealers than he is? He stole your brothers phone didnt he? And my dad doesnt like him. Im not worryed. And anyway the battle is going to start in a couple of hours. That major will be so busy he wont have time to come and complain about us."

She took a breath.

"So the war starts at a time," I said. "I didnt know that."

"9 oclock," she said. "Youll hear the cannon."

She sounded totally cool talking about a war starting. I was scared. I didnt want to show her tho. So I tried to be cool.

Then my pocket xploded.

IT DIONT REELY

but thats what it felt like. One minute nothing—
and then a buzzing and shaking that made my leg
jump like my pocket was full of bees.

"AHHH!" I shouted.

Then I remembered about being cool.

"I mean—aha aha," I said. Trying not to blush.
Witch is impossible.

And I took out the brite yellow phone. It was
buzzing. Spencer had it on silent so Grampa
wuldnt hear it. I stared at it. Shuld I anser?
About the only thing in the world I knew for

sure was that this call wuld not be for me. Wuld Spencer want me to pick up? No he wuldnt.

The buzzing stopped after a bit and I stared at the phone.

Wow.

Remember this was a few years ago when there werent as many phones as there are now. Now babies have phones. But back then holding a phone made me feel like a super hero. The world in my hand. I culd talk to any body from any where. I culd text. I culd play games. I culd—well you know this stuff. It may not seem like so much now but it was pretty cool then.

Beth was giggling.

"You freaked out," she said.

"Maybe a little," I said. "I was surprised."

I put the phone in my pocket carefully. I didnt want to drop it now.

"Where are we?" I asked. "I want to get this back to Spencer."

"I know where your tents are," she said. "I can show you."

Her hand touched mine as we walked along—just a brush from her fingers to my fingers. There was a lot wrong with the world rite now. Canada was about to go to war with America and I was a thief. But even tho there was wrong stuff I liked the feel of Beths fingers.

You can feel good even tho a lot of things.

Tyler popped out of the woods and walked back wards facing us. I cant do that without falling down but he culd. The look on his face said—trouble.

"Whats wrong?" said Beth.

He pointed to the side and behind us. The trouble was back there.

"You 2 go," I said. "I want to find my brother."

Tyler pointed at the sky and moved his finger to show the sun going higher.

"OK I will look for you guys later," I said.

I sure hoped I wuld see them again. But today was the battle. Anything culd happen.

Tyler led Beth away and I kept going along the path.

Next stop—our camp site. Wherever that was. I started walking.

* * *

A while later the sun was way over the horizon and people were getting up and I was still looking for the camp site. I was lost. This wasnt weerd—in fact it was normal. I get lost pretty often. I wasnt lost yesterday mostly because Beth and Tyler were with me. But now I was. I culd smell coffee and bacon and the smoke from a lot of camp fires. But not our fire. I didnt even know if we had a fire. I saw people's faces I knew from the day before. But not Spencer or Grampa.

I didnt panic about being lost. The first time you go on the subway its a big deal. But not the 100th time.

I decided to keep going in the same direction I was walking—away from the sunrise so the shadows stayed ahead. If I kept walking toward my shadow Id hit the paved road—rite?

Last nite Id followed it to our camp. Maybe I culd do it again.

I saw the American family with the kids who grabbed my legs. The dad was making breakfast. The boy waved at me. I waved back. I culdnt hate him even if he was the enemy. I wondered if he wuld die in the fite today. I hoped not.

I kept going.

There was a plane in the sky. Sorry—that sounds stupid. Where else wuld it be? I mean I looked up thru the trees and saw the white cloud trail behind the plane. Was it going to drop bombs? THAT made my heart go bump. I ran til I hit the road.

Rite or left? I found a loonie in my pocket. Heads rite tails left. I looked—heads. I went rite. After a minute I knew the loonie was wrong. The road dipped and I saw a red tent Id never seen before. Also the woman with the camera. So I turned back.

A few minutes later I recognized our stuff. Our tent was empty.

"Spencer!" I called. "SPENCER!"

Nothing. He was gone. Grampas tent was empty 2. His sleeping bag was there and the book he was reading and that was all.

The book title made me laff—sort of. *BILLION DOLLAR BRAIN*. Was this the grandson he wanted to have—1 with an expensive brain? The guy on the cover had glasses like Spencer. Maybe Spencers brain wuld cost a billion dollars. Mine wuldnt tho. The book about me wuld be *$1.99 BRAIN*. Funny—sort of.

"Bernard!"

Grampas voice.

"Bernard are you there? I heard you shouting!"

I came out of his tent.

"Hi Grampa! Its me. Where are you?"

HE WAS IN THE PARKING LOT.

He had a rag and a plastic bag in his hand. The doors of the Jeep were open.

"A raccoon got in," he told me. "Darn thing ate our food and smeared it over the seats. Sorry I cant offer you much breakfast. Do you want a chocolate bar? I got it for Irene but shes getting her own breakfast."

Who says no to candy? "Thank you," I said.

He tossed it to me. I recognized the face on the rapper.

"Laura Secord," I said. "They talked about her last nite."

"She was in the battle today," he said. "Her and her cow."

"But the battle hasnt started yet," I said.

The bar tasted like marshmallows. Not my favorite. But I was hungry. And even a bad candy bar is still a candy bar. Grampa leaned away from me to wipe the car seats. His back side where he bent over was bony and stiff.

"I hope you enjoy the battle Bernard," he said. "War is part of our history."

"But war with America?" I said. "Theyre bigger than us. And theyre our friends."

"They are now," he said.

"But not at 9 oclock eh?" I said. "Then theyre our enemies."

He looked back at me with a smile.

"Thats rite Bernard. At 9 oclock America becomes the enemy. And Laura Secord saves the day."

I didnt see how candy culd save the day but it sure didnt hurt.

"Whats wrong Bernard?"

"Nothing," I said.

"You sure? You jumped."

"No no. Im fine Grampa."

What happened is my pocket xploded again. But I culdnt tell Grampa about Spencers phone. Good thing it was quiet.

He finished tidying the Jeep and put the garbage bag in the big can near by. The parking lot was full of trucks and cars. There was even an ambulance. I guess that made sense—people got hurt in wars. We walked back to the camp site together.

"I havent seen much of you this trip Bernard," he said. "I hope you and your brother have had fun. And I hope youve learned things."

I nodded. Id learned that grownups can lie. They can tell you they dont have a phone when they do.

"Whats going to happen after the war?" I asked.

"After? Maybe we culd go to brunch," said Grampa. "And then home."

"All of us?" I said. "But what if somebody— what if—what if one of us gets—"

I didnt know how to say it.

"Lost?" said Grampa. "Is that what you ment? I hope that doesnt happen. I dont want to lose ether you or Spencer."

Lost ment killed. So and so was lost in the battle. Funny how Grampa didnt talk about himself getting killed. It was us he was thinking about. I guess because we were kids with our hole future ahead of us. And because hed been thru wars before.

"Just be careful Bernard," said Grampa. "Youll be fine if your careful. Stay with me if you like. I plan on enjoying the battle. Itll be fun—noisy and busy. Therell be guns and smoke and people dying all over the place."

He smiled like this was a big joke. I gulped.

"Dont worry," he said again. "If we get separated go to the log cabin where we met yesterday. That's Irenes place—Mrs Steel you know? I already told Spencer. We will all meet there after the battle and then pack up and drive off."

I nodded. Easy for him to be brave. He was old.

Spencers phone went off again and I jumped a bit. Grampa put out a hand and ruffled my hair.

"Your a funny young man Bernard," he said. "I dont know whats going on in that head of yours."

He sure didnt.

We stopped at the row of blue plastic bath-rooms. War or no war people had to pee. There were lines in front of most of the stalls. Nervous people. I didnt blame them—I was nervous and I wasnt even a real soldier. I looked around for the 1 arm guy as I washed my hands. I knew I did the rite thing taking the phone from him. But being rite isnt as important as being strong and he was bigger than me.

I looked for Spencer. Geez that brother of mine was hard to help. I wanted to give him his phone so hed stop worrying and I culdnt find him.

I saw a lot of other people. Every body pees. I saw the fiddler with the top hat. I saw my old doctor. Close up it was him all rite. Dr Jin. He nodded at me—hes a frendly guy. The soap bottle was empty when he squeezed it.

"Tomato!" he said.

I saw Beths uncle Jolon. He wore a red uniform coat today. He looked at me kind of sharp. I told him the soap squeezer was empty so he got another one and used it and took off.

Then Irene came out—I mean Mrs Steel. She smiled widely at me.

"BUNNY!" she said.

Id forgotten how loud she talked. She still had her long dress and floppy hat.

"Hi Mrs Steele—Irene," I said.

"IS DAVID WITH YOU?"

She used a lot of soap. Foam all over her arms.

"Grampas in the bathroom," I said.

"I WILL WAIT FOR HIM. ARE YOU LOOKING FORWARD TO THE BATTLE?"

The lines of people were staring at us. I didnt want to say I was scared.

"Uhh—" I said.

And then something happened inside me. It happened when the nearest bathroom door opened and Beth came out crying.

I SAID GOODBYE TO IRENE AND RAN OVER.

"Whats wrong?" I asked.

Beth wiped her eyes. "Im so upset."

"Is it Clod?"

I dont know why I said that.

"What?" she said. "Clod who? No its Dad. Come with me Bunny."

I maybe shuld of waited for Grampa but I wanted to help Beth. *Clod who?* She didnt even remember him. I wuld of smiled but I was still upset about her crying.

"See you later," I said to Irene.

"WHAT?"

I waved. Who knows what she thot I said.

On our way to their camp, Beth xplaned her dads problem.

His sord was gone.

"The one he was polishing yesterday?" I said. "The old cool one?"

"Weve looked all over the camp site and we cant find it," she said. "It was here yesterday and now its gone. Culd you look? You found the phone."

I was trying to think. Her hand on my arm made it harder for me—even harder than usual.

"What if somebody took the sord?" I said. "And thats why its gone. That 1 arm guy wants it. Remember? And he hates your dad."

"But he hasnt been here to steal it. And you went thru his tent this morning and didnt find the sord."

"Oh yah," I said.

I wuld of noticed a sord.

"Please find it Bunny. My dad likes it a lot. Please find my dads sord."

Beths hand was cool and dry. My heart bumped inside my chest.

*   *   *

Mr Tecumseth had fresh paint on his face. He said it was nice to see me again. "But we must go soon. The battle is about to start."

He turned away to get on a horse that somebody held for him.

"Can Bunny look for your sord?" asked Beth. "Hes good at finding things."

Mr Tecumseth smiled down from the horses back. "If Bunny stays here he will miss the battle," he said. "You cant ask him to do that."

"I dont mind," I said. "I dont like fiting that much. I will try to find your sord sir."

Uncle Jolon held onto Mr Tecumseths horse. His big nose came down and his big chin came up when he frowned at me. He said something to Beth. She said something back. He got on his own horse and rode away after Mr Tecumseth.

"I dont think your uncle Jolon likes me," I said.

"Forget him. Hes an old grump who doesnt like any body," she said. "He hates Daddy for going to university to study history. And for doing this Indian hero stuff on weekends. Uncle Jolon doesnt usually come out. I dont know why hes here now."

Somebody far away made an announcement. I culdnt make out the words.

Beth culd. "The battles about to start!" she said. "I have to go."

"Your fiting?" I said.

"Dad said I culd. Isnt it great?"

She was like Grampa—she thot war was fun.

"Tylers already there. Listen—when you find the sord sneak onto the battle field. Give Dad the sord. None of the other Indians has one."

I had to ask. Id been thinking it all along.

"Wuldnt a gun be better than a sord?" I said. "Or a tank or a bazooka or something? This is a war. Sords are cool but—"

She laffed.

"Your a riot Bunny," she said. "A bazooka! Yah. Thatd be perfect."

I didnt think she was making fun of me. She reely thot I was a riot. Well at least she wasnt crying any more.

"OK. How do I find the battle field?" I asked. She was already hurrying off.

"Follow the noise," she called over her sholder.

I never got a chance to look for the sord. Not for a second. I took a couple of steps into the camp site and then I herd a horse coming. You know the sound a horses feet make on the ground—*thuba thub thuba thub thuba thub*? That one. I looked up. The horse was big and coming fast. It jumped off the path and headed rite at the camp site—rite at me. And guess who was riding it?

Rite. He must of been on his way to the battle field. Now he was on his way to me. He was a good rider—he didnt need a hand on the rains. He held a whip in his 1 hand and steered with his knees. His mustash stuck out like a banner.

When he came close to me he leaned over and slashed with his whip. I ducked. His horse *thuba thubbed* past me. And then turned around.

What culd I do? Even if there was a police officer right there what culd I do? The war was about to start and war is bigger than police.

I did the only thing possible.

I ran.

THE NEXT BIT OF THE DAY

was a nite mare—the kind where the monster gets closer and closer. The 1 arm man was the monster. I went zig zag zig thru the trees with the monster right behind me and got ahead. Then I crawled thru a hedge and the monster jumped over it and almost got me. I screamed.

I dont know if this took 2 minutes or 20. It seemed like hours.

He shouted at me from the back of the horse. Called me stupid—witch was maybe rite but not nice.

Then he called me a thief. Wuld you beleeve it?

I know you are but what am I? I didnt say that but I culd of. I kept running.

The place was empty—I didnt see a single Canadian soldier. No one to help me. I ran thru trees that were 2 close together for a horse to fit. I got ahead of the 1 arm man and came to a hill. I ran down as fast as I culd.

Man I was scared. Grampa talked about how much fun war culd be. This wasnt any fun at all. I guess I was a coward.

I came to a big red tent with letters on it. *NC.* North Something. Or New Something. Or Not Something. Whatever. *NC.* A woman stood in front of the tent in an old timey dress and bonnet. She looked kind of like Irene only skinny. She was the first person Id seen in a while.

"Help!" I shouted as I ran past her. What I ment was that the 1 arm man wuld be coming soon and she shuld watch out. But I was 2 scared and tired to say anything but help.

The flap was open and I ran thru it. Inside the tent there were people carrying movy cameras and poles and other things. I stopped and took long breaths.

I was happy to see every body but I was still scared. A woman with glasses and a pad and pen came over to ask what I wanted. She was so calm she made me feel bad. Like I shuld be doing better and not being so scared. I tried to xplaen.

"Sorry Im a—"

I tried to say coward. But I was out of breath so I culdnt say it all.

"Im a cow," I said. "A cow…a cow…"

I was puffing so hard I culdnt finish. The woman nodded happily.

"I thot you werent coming," she said. "I thot Id have to do it. But here you are. Great."

I was surprised.

"What?" I said.

"Get in. I will help."

"What?" I said again.

She gave me a pair of baggy white pants and told me to put them on. OK I thot. If I change clothes the 1 arm man mite not know me. The woman ran to the door of the tent and waved. Then she got out her phone and punched a number.

"We are good to go here," she said. "The back end showed up after all. Hes in costume now."

"What?" I said again—and then I got it. Finally. These were not white pants with black blotches. This was a cow costume.

There was shouting in the distance. The war was starting. And I was the back end of a cow.

Dont laff OK?

The front end—my front end—walked in the tent. Funny to see a 2 legged cow.

"You," it said to me. With a shake of its horns.

"Quiet," said the woman. "We have to get you on the battle field."

The two ends of the cow fit together with buttons. The woman with the short hair did them up and there I was—bent over and pretty much in the dark. And everything smelled bad. I put my hands out and found the sholders of my front half.

"Hi," I said. "Im Bunny."

"I know who you are," he said. The voice was familiar even tho he was whispering.

"Clod?"

"Yah. And your Beths friend who cant ride a horse."

"Shhh!" said the woman with the phone. "Quiet you guys."

She told us to walk forward. "Left leg first," she said. "Front half leads and back half follows. OK? Lets get out of here. Go."

Clod said, "Left—rite—left—rite" and we clumped forward. It was briter now that we were outside. I culd see my arms. It still smelled like wool and dirt and Clod.

Bleck.

"Out of my way you idiot!" came a loud shout from up ahead of us. I culdnt see him but I knew who it was.

"Hey!" said the woman. "Watch where your going!"

Thuba thub. Thuba thub. Stop.

"Im Major Brasher. Im a reactor! You get out of my way!"

I choked.

"Left—rite—left," whispered Clod. My hands on his sholders were shaking.

"Im chasing a thief," said the 1 arm man. "A stupid kid in a blue shirt. He headed this way. Who are you?"

"Im with the film unit. This is Laura Secords cow."

The 1 arm man snorted. Or maybe the horse did. I culdnt tell.

"And here comes Laura. In the bonnet."

"She looks stupid," said the 1 arm man. "So does that cow."

Thuba thub. Thuba thub. He was gone.

I didnt understand any of this. Laura Secord was candy. Reactors were scary. We were about to fite the strongest country in the world.

The 1 arm man was an enemy. And I was inside a cow costume with Clod. Confusing or what?

Now something else was going on. Clod bent his head and sholders lower. I heard a clanking sound. Like hitting a pot. The film woman said something to Laura Secord—I culdnt hear what or what Laura said back.

"Ready to march?" said Clod. "Lets go. Left—rite—left—"

BOOM!

That HAD to be a cannon going off. It was way louder than a gun shot or a bunch of gun shots.

The war had started.

YOUVE SEEN THE MOVYS

so you know what war looks like. Capturing that hill. Saving that private. Blowing up that bridge. Sinking that ship. Youve seen jets zooming. Blood flowing. Youve seen planes and tanks and xplosions. Sweat and tears and frend-ship. And youve seen the dead bodies—all the dead bodies.

My war didnt look like that. Not any part of that. My war was dim and small. I couldnt see anything apart from the back of Clods shirt and the top of my arms. And the inside of the cow suit. I felt my way forward like a blind guy with Clod as my seeing eye dog. I herd guns going off but I didnt know where they were. I herd shouting but it all sounded like *waa waa waa*. I herd the pot clang sound whenever we hit a bump—there was a bell around the cows neck. I was scared and everything smelled bad. Some of the smell was smoke. Some was cow. Some was Clod. And some was me.

One good thing—we culd talk. Nobody wuld hear us over the noise of battle.

"This is all wrong," said Clod. "There was supposed to be a real cow."

"At least we arent getting killed," I said. "Americans dont make war on cows."

"This costume stinks," said Clod. "My mom will be mad."

"What about Beth," I said. "Will she be mad?"

I dont know why I asked about her. I culdnt help it.

"Beth who? Oh you mean the native girl?" He laffed. "Shes already mad. She threw the end of her ice cream cone at me when I called her Pocahontas. Hey we go downhill here. Careful."

I didnt like Clod making fun of Beth. I was glad she threw the ice cream. Then I wondered why I thot about Beth so much. I dont understand myself sometimes. Actually a lot of times. Thats what happens when you have a $1.99 brain.

"My mom will be happy to see me," I said. "If I ever get home."

Spencers phone went off again. That was like the 4th time.

"Do you want to get that?" asked Clod. "I can feel it vibrating thru your arms."

"Oh," I said.

And I thot—maybe I SHULD get it. What if it was Mom or Dad calling Spencer? What if there was important news?

"Nobody can see you here," said Clod. "Luther wont yell at you."

Luther? Oh yah. That guy. He would of said phones were farb.

"Go on," said Clod. "The ground is pretty flat up ahead."

So I took out Spencers phone.

When I pushed some buttons a lite went on. Now I culd see what I had to do. *PULL TO UNLOCK* it said.

Before I culd do that the lite flashed and the phone rang really loud. Oops. I pushed some more buttons and the ringing stopped.

"Sorry," I said to Clod.

"Thats OK," he said.

Now I pulled to unlock the phone. And everything changed.

All rite not everything. But a few important things.

* * *

WHERE R U?

That was the last message. Before that was another.

WHERE R U?

The one before that was *WHY U NOT REPLY?* And the one before that was *WHERE R U?* again. The messages were all from somebody named J.

Oh oh I thot—Spencer was in trouble.

Clang!

"Ouch," said Clod. "Laura Secord just tripped and yanked on the rope."

I wondered who J culd be. Dads name was Jerry.

"Coming to some woods," said Clod. "The ground is a bit bumpy."

I checked farther up the texts to see if J was Dad. I know I shudnt of done this—phones are private. But still. A few texts up was one from early this morning.

GOT SORD—HID IN HOLLOW BIRCH.

I had a funny prickly feeling—like swet going down your back. I scrolled farther up. And found a text from Spencer.

MEET YOU IN FIELD BY HOLLOW BIRCH TREE 3:00.

"You OK?" said Clod.

"No," I said.

THIS WASNT
SPENCERS PHONE.

It was the same kind of phone. It had the same cover. It unlocked the same way. It looked exactly like Spencers. But it wasnt his. Spencer culdnt of sent a message yesterday at 3. He didnt have this phone.

Who did? Who did I see in the field by the birch tree yesterday at 3 o'clock?

This was the 1 arm mans phone.

Woe!

Wow!

Oops!

I was a reel thief. I thot I was stealing my brothers phone back—witch was OK. But I wasnt stealing BACK. I was just stealing. That wasnt OK—that was terrible.

These thots went thru my mind in a second. I felt myself getting hot.

Then I thot—wait. I thot—what is going on?

I put the texts in the rite order.

First this guy J and the 1 arm guy met in the field with the hollow birch tree. Then J got a sord. Then he hid the sord in the birch tree. And now the sord was in the tree waiting for the 1 arm guy to get it.

I didnt know who J was but the sord just HAD to be Mr Tecumseths. The 1 arm man wanted it. And it was missing. So what I shuld do now was—

"I have to get out," I said to Clod. "Where are we?"

"What?"

"What can you see?"

"Uhh—woods," he said. "I can see woods."

"Are there any Americans around?"

"I dont think so. Laura Secord led her cow past the battle—rite?"

I had no idea what he was talking about. I held the phone up so I culd see in the dimness and started fumbling at the buttons of the cow costume.

"What are you doing?" said Clod.

Three buttons later the cow came apart and I stepped out of the back half.

We were at the edge of the woods. There was an open field off to the left. Gun shots and shouts came from over there. That was the battle. And smoke rolling like fog only it smelled like fire crackers. Clod was still walking in the front half of the cow. I saw his shirt and pants and the back of bonnet girl—the one they called Laura Secord. She was pulling on a rope.

It was silly for Clod to keep going without me. He let the bonnet girl keep pulling and stepped backwards out of his cow suit. The girl didnt look back—didnt even notice. Smoke rolled thru and she was gone.

*   *   *

First thing Clod did was spit. He did it over and over. I forgot that about him—he must of missed spitting inside the cow.

I thot hed be mad at me but no. He came up to me with a smile.

"I was sure sick of that costume," he said. "What a stink eh? I guess the film crew will use what they have."

I didnt think the news guys wuld focus on us. War was bigger than cows. And there was a reel battle going on over to the left. Thats where the hollow birch tree wuld be. Witch was where Mr Tecumseths sord was. Witch was where I had to go.

I started forward and had to stop when a horse almost ran me down.

Nobody was riding it. It ran away and then stopped and looked back. Smoke rolled past it. Clod put 2 fingers to his mouth and did one of those whistles. The horse took a step toward us. Then stopped again.

"Hey there Dancer," Clod said to it. "How are you doing boy?"

He waved his hand slowly in the air like he was about to do a magic trick. The horse watched. Clod spit—a gentle *patooee* sound. He walked toward the horse spitting some more. I cot up to him.

"Dont run," he said to me reel low. "Dont spook the horse. Hey Dancer," he said in a louder voice. "Looks like you lost your rider eh boy?"

I found myself watching Clods twisting hand. Clod walked up to the horse talking all the time. The horse and I watched his hand.

"Walk around the horse," Clod said in his low voice. "And grab the rains from the other side. Dont get close and dont move fast."

His hand was making figure 8s in the air. Around it went. Round and round.

"Bunny?"

Round and round and round.

"Bunny did you hear what I just said?"

"Huh? I mean yes."

Clod was waving his hand slowly all this time. "Stay calm and get the rains," he told me. "Dancer shuldnt be out here by himself."

What about us? I thot. Why worry about horses when people were shooting?

"When we get Dancer safe we can ride him together."

Now THAT was a good idea. Because I had to—

"Do it Bunny. Itll be easy," said Clod. And it was. He talked and moved his hand in the air and I walked around the horse. I stayed calm by counting the times Clods hand went round and round and round and round and round and when I was on the far side of the horse I took the rains in my hand. Clod moved in front of the horse and grabbed the rains from me and got in the saddle like going upstairs. Easy as that.

When the horse felt Clod on his back he calmed rite down. Clod gave me his hand and pulled hard. In a minute I was sitting behind him on the horses wide brown back.

I told him where to ride.

"The birch tree?" he said. "Why?"

"Theres a sord in it. I have to find it."

"But your dressed wrong for the battle. Look at that shirt."

"I have to do it," I said again. "And no body will see me in this smoke anyway."

"Well thats true. But theres lots of traffic."

"Do it Clod," I said. "Its important."

You know THAT voice—the one people have to listen to and do what you say? Every body has that voice inside them. It comes from believing something.

"Ride to the tree Clod," I said in that voice. And he listened.

"Lets see how close we can get," he said. "Hang on tite."

He kicked Dancer in the side. I hugged Clod around the waist as we *thuba thubbed* toward the battle field.

"Whats wrong with my shirt anyway?" I asked. "My dad says its groovy."

CLOD WAS AMAZING.

He raced the horse thru the smoke. He kept away from the troops. He jumped over ditches. He turned left to look for the birch tree—then rite—then left again. You know the way the getaway driver loses the police cars? Clod was my getaway driver. I hung on to him like grip tape. How did Beth say she knew him—some kind of twisty horse racing? I believed it.

"Thanks a lot for doing this," I said.

He didnt owe me anything. I didnt used to like him. In fact I wanted to kill him with an ax. Not reely but sort of. And then—well—I didnt.

He was the front half of my cow and being an OK guy. And now he was riding into danger to help me. And I was kind of liking him. Weerd.

"Hey no problem. This is fun," he shouted. Like we were a couple of pals riding around and having crazy adventures. Bunny and Clod.

We passed lots of fiting. I saw blue and red uniforms and horses. I saw guys loading and firing their guns and guys charging at other guys and guys waving sords and hats. Every body was covered in smoke. So this was war. I didnt have time to worry tho. I had something to do.

I saw the rocky hill with the steps cut into it where Id seen the 1 arm man talking to the mistery guy yesterday. J the mistery guy. If the hill was here then the birch tree must be over there. I pointed and Clod turned the horse.

The birch tree popped out of the smoke like your knee pops out of the bubble bath. You cant see it—and then you can. I shouted. Clod pulled on the rains. Dancer the horse stopped.

I patted Clod on the sholder and slid myself backwards. I landed on my feet and ran.

Ever searched a hollow tree for a sord? No? Well heres what NOT to do. Dont go around it tapping the trunk. Dont look for an opening at eye level. Dont clime up to check for hidey holes. I did all this stuff and didnt find anything.

Look down low. Thats where the hiding place is. Look at the bottom of the trunk. Get down on your knees. Therell be a skinny crack down there that fits the sord perfectly. Slide in your hand and find the sord in its thing—what do they call that? The rapper the sord comes in that hangs onto your belt sheath.

Now you have the sord—NOW is when you clime the tree. You want to see the big picture so you can decide where to take your sord.

I did that. Clod helped me up on Dancer then held me steady so I culd clime. I stood up on a heavy low branch and saw the battle in bits and pieces in between smoke clouds.

It was smaller than youd think considering we were fiting America. This looked more like a football game. Blues and reds. A lot of shoving like in football. Xept I saw a red guy lift his gun and shoot a blue guy who threw his hands in the air and fell down. That was gross. I looked away—and there was Mr Tecumseth! I only saw him for a second. He was on a bit of a hill pointing at something with blue uniforms all around. Then the smoke covered him. I got down.

Wait—something was wrong with Dancer. He stood with his front leg bent and his foot in the air. Hoof I mean. Clod stood next to him.

"His shoe came off," said Clod. "Its no big deal but he has to go back to the core al. Sorry I cant help you any more Bunny."

He walked away. Dancer limped after him swishing his black tail. The smoke rolled in and they were gone. Both of them. I never saw them again.

Funny guy Clod. More worryed about a horse shoe than getting shot.

I headed to where I thot Mr Tecumseth was. Smoke and gun fire all over the place. Soldiers stared at me.

"Has the siren gone?" asked a guy in red. I didnt know what he ment.

I culdnt see anything. Hoped I was going the rite way. But maybe I wasnt.

Funny eh? I had the sord. I was ready to save the day. But I culdnt find my way. Imagine if Saint George culdnt find the dragon. Imagine if Prince Charming culdnt find whats her name with the long hair. Not that I was a prince or saint. But still.

Im used to getting lost. I didnt panic. I kept walking. Counting my steps. 223 224 225. Tap on my sholder and who dyou think it was? Rite.

"Tyler!" I said. "How did you find me?"

He pulled something out of his belt. Not the tomahawk—the old telescope.

"So you were looking for me," I said.

He grinned and clapped when he saw the sord. Then he grabbed my arm and pulled.

We went past blue and red troops shoving each other. The smoke was so thick I culdnt see any thing. It was nite in the middle of the day.

And there was the 1 arm man! I only saw his back but I knew it was him. He had one of those huge pistols. I screamed and ran forward.

"Hey!" I shouted. And I wasnt thinking about what horses ate.

"Leave Beth alone!" I shouted.

Thats who he was pointing his pistol at. I know eh? A grown man and a kid. Not cool. I took the sord out of its rapper. It felt lite and springy in my hand.

He turned. His mouth went wide when he saw me. His big mustash quivered.

"You!" he shouted.

He turned and aimed his gun at my face. I swung the sord.

He fired.

I DIDNT DIE.

Well you know that—Im writing this story and its years later. Anyway. I dont know how the 1 arm man missed me. He must of been a lousy shot. I clanged something hard with the sord. My hand stung like it does when you get a hit off the wrong part of the baseball bat. Then the smoke cleared and this was what I saw.

Me and Beth and the 1 arm man and Mr Tecumseth were in the middle of a circle of soldiers. Red and blue and brown with frinj— some of the First Nations soldiers werent in uniform. A little ways away was a guy with a news camera. I culdnt believe how close he was to the fiting.

One of the soldiers laffed. He was looking at us. Then another one laffed. And another. Soon they were all laffing. Beth laffed too. Mr Tecumseth was having trouble keeping his face strait.

"What?" shouted the 1 arm man. He was angry. He stared around the circle. "What is wrong with you all? The redcoats havent won yet! And this savage is pathetic—look at him! He doesnt even have a sord. How can he command without a sord?"

His gun was on the ground—that was the clangy thing Id hit. He pointed at Mr Tecumseth— a smaller man with a fether in his hair.

"You savage! Call yourself a leader?" he sneered. "Where is your—your—"

His voice died away to a little croak.

"Oh no," he finished.

Because now Mr Tecumseth had his sord back. I gave it to him as soon as the smoke cleared. It was in his hand like it had been there all along.

One of the fiters near us had a tomahawk. That was his weapon. He stared at Mr Tecumseths sord like it was a ghost. He said something in Mohawk—I guess—and then said it again in English. He was talking to the 1 arm man.

"You did not find the sord," he said.

This was Beths uncle—the one who hated me. Uncle Jolon. As soon as I thot of his name I knew.

"Your J," I said. Loud enuff for him to hear.

J for Jolon.

"You stole your brothers sord," I said.

He looked at the 1 arm man and then at me and then back at the 1 arm man. He probly didnt mean to say anything but he was so surprised he culdnt help himself.

"How did HE get it?" Uncle Jolon asked the 1 arm man. HE meaning me. "I told YOU where it was."

He dropped his tomahawk. The American soldier beside him didnt hit him. He was too busy laffing.

The 1 arm man was upset. His plan had fallen apart. He was hoping to make fun of Mr Tecumseth and now that wasnt happening. No body was laffing at Mr Tecumseth. They were all laffing at him. And he didnt know why.

I knew why.

He had only half a mustash. That was why. Remember Mr Tecumseth sharpening his sord? I must of hit the 1 arm mans mustash on my way down to his gun. The sord was so sharp it shaved him. Now he had a rich full blond mustash on one side of his nose and a little squiggle on the other side. He looked reely funny.

Mr Tecumseth stepped toward him waving the sord in small circles.

"Yield Yankee," he said in that deep voice of his. Then he culdnt help himself and started to laff along with every body else.

A siren went off in the distance. Not the *boop-boop* kind of siren—the long whining kind. *RRRrrrrrrrrrrrr.*

"The wars over!" Beth yelled.

188

Rite away every body relaxed.

Beth ran over and gave me a hug. Reely. Then she hugged her dad and Tyler. Wow. She had strong arms. My body felt fizzy from her hug. Tylers smile was wide and white. It was a good smile.

The soldiers were shaking hands. Reds and blues. Long hats and tall hats and fethers. Every body was shaking hands with every body else. The camera guy was packing up his stuff.

It happened so fast. One minute every body was fiting and the next they were talking and laffing like theyd never been enemies. You know the way hockey teams shake hands after the buzzer? Like that. I guess war is more like hockey than you think.

*   *   *

The war was over. I felt this heavy thing lifting off me and I didnt even know I was carrying it. War I guess. And I culd still feel Beths hug. Wow.

Mr Tecumseth took a deep breath and turned to his brother. "Come here," he said.

When ever anybody looked at the 1 arm man they laffed. Even his own guys. He shook his head and marched off waving his hands. He didnt get it. Just didnt get it. He was like me in math class trying to understand about even and odd numbers. (I still dont reely get them—theyre all odd numbers to me.) I felt kind of sorry for him until I remembered that he shot at me. Then I didnt feel so bad.

Uncle Jolon wasnt laffing. His head was down and he was listening to his brother. I dont know the words Mr Tecumseth was saying but I didnt have to. I remembered what Beth told me about her grumpy uncle. I guess he took the sord because he wanted to make his brother look bad. Jolon was still grumpy but now he was scared. Mr Tecumseth was shorter than his brother but he looked bigger. He was the boss. He pointed off the field and his brother went with his tomahawk dangling.

The camera guy came up to me.

"You and the American major—did you 2 plan that mustash bit? It was great."

I shook my head.

"What are you doing here anyway?" he said. "Your not a reactor. Howd you even get on the field?"

I didnt get it. I didnt know what he ment by reactors.

"I was a cow," I said.

"What?"

"Then I was on a horse. And then I got lost til Tyler saw me in his telescope."

The camera guy frowned. Now he didnt get it.

People came across the field and down the rocky steps. They were watching the war—like hockey fans. They carried phones and cameras. I looked for Spencer and Grampa but culdnt see them. I did see the little round guy with the fiddle. And one of the guys with 1 eye. And Dr Jin.

Everyone wanted to talk to Mr Tecumseth. He was still upset about his brother—I culd tell. He watched him walk off the field. But he smiled for the cameras and showed his sord. Beth made hand moves and talked like a machine gun.

The sun was high and hot and the air was clear. I was getting used to the idea of not being at war. Tyler came up with a bucket of water for me. He looked at the bucket and then at my face. I guess I was pretty grimy.

"Thanks," I said.

He shook his head like—No problem. I washed my face and hands. The water in the bucket got pretty black. Tyler and I looked at each other.

"I live in Toronto," I said. "Do you?"

He shook his head.

"Close to Toronto?"

He shook his head again. We looked at each other some more. Then he nodded. I knew what he was saying.

"Yah," I said. "Me too."

Beth came up and it was nite and day because she didnt stop talking for a minute or two. She put a hand on each of our sholders.

"You guys are my favorites," she said. "My all time favorites." That made me feel good. Tyler poked me. I told him to shut up. He poked me again.

Mr Tecumseth shook my hand for a long time. He thanked me for finding his sord before the end of the battle. I wanted to say I was sorry about his brother but I didnt know how. And anyway it wasnt my business.

"You were a hero," Mr Tecumseth told me.

There was one thing I had wanted to ask ever since the fiting ended.

"Who won?"

He smiled. "Today we did," he said.

"Good," I said.

But I wondered what he ment by *today*. Wuld there be another war soon? I hoped not. I reely hoped not.

I headed off with Beth and Tyler. I wanted them to meet my brother. Spencer wuld like both of—

"Wait," I said.

HOW CULD I FORGET
ABOUT THE 1 ARM MAN?

I still had his phone! I had to give it back. Mind you he shot me in the face last time he saw me. Before that he chased me with a whip.

"Come with me," I said to Beth and Tyler.

He stood by himself in the middle of the battle field with his hand up to his eyes to block the sun. He squinted into the distance. He didnt look at us rite away.

"Any of you seen a big bay horse?" he asked. "He spooked and threw me in the fite. Ran off. I dont want to lose him."

"You mean Dancer?" I said. "Dancer was *your* horse?"

Did I know that already? Maybe I shuld of. But I was surprised.

The 1 arm man turned and saw us. And frowned like thunder. "You know Dancer?"

"Clod took him back to the core al," I said. "He was limping because he lost a shoe. A horse shoe I mean." In case he thot I ment a sandal or a running shoe. "Clod said it was no big deal."

The 1 arm man kept frowning. "You," he growled at me. "You little moron. Your all over the place arent you. Every time I turn around there you are."

I didnt like being called names. But words dont matter as much as what happens. This guy didnt have the sord and he didnt win the battle.

"Im sorry I took your phone this morning," I said. It felt funny to say sorry to a guy who called me names and shot at me. "I didnt know it was yours when I took it. I thot it was my brothers. Here you go."

I took the brite yellow case out of my pocket.

"What?" said Beth. "What? Thats not your brothers? We went to all that trouble and it wasnt your brothers phone? Oh Bunny! Thats amazing. Dont you think so Tyler? I sure do. Wowee. So that looks like your brothers phone eh? Same case. Yah I can see how you would—"

The 1 arm man grabbed the phone and opened it. He scrolled thru the texts and started to swear. I guess he was thinking how different everything culd of been.

It was hard to look at him without laffing. Half of a big mustash makes your face look reely funny. I didnt tell him about the mustash. Hed find out in time.

I was glad I wasnt alone. He was a mean guy and he hated me. But everything is OK if your friends are with you—even getting yelled at.

The three of us headed across the field side by side by side. Beth who culdnt stop talking and Tyler who didnt talk at all and me. I was in the middle. Looking ahead thru a break in the crowd I saw a flash of baggy shorts and skinny legs. Was that Spencer? I hoped so. I never did find his phone. Witch is funny when you think how hard I looked for it. Maybe getting what you want isnt the most important thing. Maybe messing up can work for you 2. I dont know. I tried my best and found out some true things. Im OK with that.

And didnt a lot of weerd stuff happen in a day? I mean—a lot! Told you so. Yah, I picked the rite title for this story.

DISCLAIMER

This book deals with historical events, badly. Do not treat what you have read here as factual. I did not make up the War of 1812. Tecumseh and Laura Secord were real folks. But pretty much everything else is, well, iffy.

ACKNOWLEDGMENTS

Thanks to the Orca family, management, editorial, sales, marketing, publicity, for support, flexibility, and being open to new ideas. Thanks to the Seven family, brothers and sister writers of adventure, mystery, fun, and especially Ted Staunton, co-plotter and craziest diamond of them all.

RICHARD SCRIMGER has published twenty or so books for children and adults, and written for print media and television. His middle-school novel *The Nose from Jupiter* won the Mr. Christie's Award, and his books have appeared on the *Globe and Mail*'s and ALA's notable-books lists. He likes to live downtown, drink coffee and talk about writing—(and everything else). He usually needs a haircut and does not know what the problem is. He does not have four children—they have him. *Weerdest Day Ever!* is the prequel to *Ink Me,* Richard's novel in Seven (the series). For more information, visit www.scrimger.ca or follow him on Twitter @richardscrimger.

THE SEVEN PREQUELS

HOW IT ALL BEGAN...
7 GRANDSONS
7 JOURNEYS
7 AUTHORS
7 ASTOUNDING PREQUELS

The seven grandsons from the bestselling **Seven (the series)** and **The Seven Sequels** return in **The Seven Prequels**, along with their daredevil grandfather, David McLean

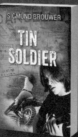

SEE WHERE BUNNY GOES NEXT IN AN EXCERPT FROM **INK ME** FROM SEVEN (THE SERIES).

AFTER IT WAS OVER

SHE SAT ME DOWN at a big table and ast if I wantd water or juice or anything.

No I said.

Or sum thing to eat—a bagel or muffin?

No.

My voys sounded funny like it was coming from behind a door. My ears were still messd up from the gunshots. She told me to rite my full name. I put down Bunny O'Toole and ast if that was OK. My names Bernard but no 1 ever calld me that xept Grampa. She said Bunny was OK.

Im Sarjent Nolan but you can call me Nikki she said. Like Nikki K the rapper—you no her dont you?

O yah I said but I dint reely.

The paper was yello with lines. The pen was the kind that went *blob blob* wen you rote. Now your address said Nikki so I put that down—2 Tecumsee. I ast did she want Trono and Canada and that. She shook her head.

And how old r you Bunny? Rite that too.

I put down 15.

You sure you dont want sum thing to eat? You look hungry.

Well mayb a muffin.

OK.

She told me to rite down what happend in my own words. I ast what she ment by my own words and she said what do you member?

Starting ware? I said.

At the start.

Like wen we got to Sure Way and the Angels and Buffalos were there with there bikes and the SUV and then the pleece cars came?

Befor that.

Like driving to the mall?

Befor that.

Lunch? That was at Snocones house. There was a baby.

Befor that.

Befor lunch—like brekfast? I had that at home I said. OJ and Rice Krisps. Spencer likes them and Mom always makes sure there there.

By now Nikki was frowning the way evry 1 does at me. Not meen but tired you no? Like she wantd to say Jeez Bunny smarten up. Guys do that even if they all reddy no Im a dummy. Not Spencer but evry 1 els. Mom and Dad do. Mom sure does. I can see it in her face. She loves me but she wants to yell at me 2.

Sorry I said. I dont no what you want.

I wishd Spencer was there to xplane for me. But Spencer was off with Dad kissing that actress and getting lost and driving Mom crazy. I was here at the pleece stashun with Nikki the cop and she was giving me the Jeez Bunny look and rolling up her blu sleevs. A sister Jaden wud call her but I cant cuz Im not reely a brother.

Start at the begining she said. Wen did you join the possy?